Broken Promises

Broken Promises

By Donna M. Zadunajsky

Copyright

ISBN: 978-1-938037-146

Book Cover Design by: Travis Miles
Interior Format by: Donna M. Zadunajsky

Connect with the Author:

http://www.donnazadunajsky.com

http://www.facebook.com/donnamzadunajsky

http://twitter.com/AuthorDonnaMZ

Reviews of Broken Promises

I just finished one of the page-turners that I love to read. BROKEN PROMISES is a very enjoyable read. I didn't want to put the book down. The author writes of characters that are very true to life... Gayle Pace

Broken Promises is a look into what it is like living with an alcoholic. You want to believe that it's the last time he will drink. You want to believe it's the last time he will cheat on you. But when is it enough? While some think Clare is weak, I found her to be pretty strong. How easy it would be to just lie there and cry? Instead she starts her own business cleaning houses and takes care of her daughter. There were some twists towards the end that I didn't see coming... Draaks

Broken Promises is the second fictional novel I've read and reviewed by Author Donna M. Zadunajsky. Although it is a fictional murder mystery for the most part, the majority of story line is very true to life and one that many people can identify with in one way or another.

Oftentimes, substance abuse whether alcohol or drugs, may lead to other forms of abuse. As so adeptly depicted in this novel, physical and emotional abuse usually follows toward a spouse. This inappropriate behavior is very difficult to embrace and will be the undoing of many a marriage as clearly demonstrated in "Broken Promises". This author paints a realistic and heart wrenching picture of the personal pain that is endured in this kind of living arrangement... Dolores Ayotte

It's been many years since I sat down and read a novel. This book was enjoying and easy to read. This book was interesting and eye opening to a life with an alcoholic. At different times, I found myself wanting to jump into the book and give the alcoholic an attitude adjustment, but I guess he got what was coming to him. I heard about how living with an alcoholic can be but now I feel like I lived with one reading this book. I'm so so happy that Clare found happiness... Rodney Giel

Prologue

Present time...

I stare into the darkness. I can just make out the white walls surrounding me. I can't remember how long I have been here in this room. Some things I don't recall because of the drugs they give me, but I have memories, which haunt me most nights, and I start to lose my mind. I guess that's why I'm in this place with white walls.

I'm not allowed to have pencils or pens or anything that is sharp and could hurt someone, but they do give me crayons to draw with. I would like to think I could adjust to the life I lead now, but when I awake from my dreams, I go crazy. *Crazy*, a word I don't like to hear or use when I'm locked up in this place. This place would make anyone insane. At least that's what they tell me anyway—that I'm insane.

I hear footsteps outside my door. A door with a tiny window just above my head, so I can't see out, but they can see in. A light clicks on, the door opens, and a man in a red smock walks in carrying a tray of food for me. It's the same man I see every day, which tells me it must be morning. The people here wear different colored smocks, which I guess is, so we can determine what time it is.

"Breakfast," the man in the red smock, says each morning. I am not able to approach him or any of the people who come into my room, or they will strap my hands and feet down onto the metal railing of the bed. I don't like them doing that, so I try to be a good girl and do as they ask.

He sets the tray on a small table in the corner of my room. It's where I eat and draw my pictures of my dreams; some are good, but most are bad. They hang them on the wall for me to look at, but they don't know what they mean to me. The people who work here tell me that the bad pictures are about the girl in my dreams — I know I was only trying to protect her, the girl in my dreams. We were once friends, so long ago in the world outside these walls.

I don't answer back when the man in the red smock talks to me. I sit and wait for him to leave, then I eat my breakfast. I have to eat the food quickly because they come back in and take away the tray if I don't. I've learned to count in my head the amount of time I have. They give me fifteen minutes to eat. I write crayon marks on the backside of my pictures for each minute. They ask me about the marks, but I don't tell them. I don't even know what day it is, much less the month or year. I guess it doesn't really matter; I'm not going anywhere.

The light clicks on and off twice to let me know that they are coming in for the tray. I quickly make my way to the bed and sit down while they take it away. A woman enters, glides over to the bed, and sits down beside me. Her blonde hair rests softly on her shoulders. I can feel her blue eyes stare through me.

"It's time for you to come with me. If you don't fight, then I won't have them stick the nasty needle in your arm that you don't like."

I nod my head at her.

She takes me to a room that is no bigger than the one I live in. In the center of the room is a large metal table with a chair on each side. A pitcher of water with two glasses sits at the far end of the table, along with a notepad and a tape recorder.

She motions me to sit down and I obey. She sits in front of me, then adjusts the tape recorder between us and presses the recorder button. I don't look at her; I just stare at the recorder on the table in front of me.

The woman takes out a pen from her pocket and scribbles something on the notepad. I can't read what she has written, but I honestly don't care.

"Okay, I want to go over the last matter we discussed. You said there was a story to tell me that went along with the pictures you have been drawing. Could you please start from the beginning and tell me all about it?" the woman asks.

I glance down at my hands that are strapped to the chair and swallow hard to keep down the food. Taking in a deep breath through my nose, I begin my story.

— "This girl that I have mentioned, the one that used to be my friend, it is her story. A story of a love so deep it would cut you like a knife." I snicker before going on. "My friend's love turned into betrayal and fear.

She doesn't understand what I did for her, but I did what I had to do for my friend to be happy again and to live a life free from fear and heartache.

One

Four years earlier…

The intercom crackled as it came to life. A woman spoke cheerfully into the microphone, "Last call for flight 352 to Ft. Myers, Florida." Clare clipped up her brunette hair and lifted Kayla onto her hip while Jim wheeled the suitcase and booster seat to the terminal.

Jim had suggested they go to Naples, Florida for Thanksgiving to see his mom and stepdad. With all the activity going on at home, Clare thought it would be a great idea to take some time away from her hectic life. She wouldn't actually *say* their hectic life because he was the one causing it. The one thing she still had was her thinking; she could think anything she wanted, and he would never know. She often wondered what went on in his head — especially because of the *crazy* things, he did.

Shifting in her seat, Kayla held on to her mom's arm and her teddy bear. People scampered down the aisle trying to find their seats. A couple of kids near the front of the plane started bickering about who was going to sit near the window. A tall beefy man told them to stop fighting and sit down.

The door shut to the plane and the plane lined up for take-off. This would be Kayla's first time flying in a plane, Clare mused, and she thought back to the doctor's appointment Kayla had a few days ago. The doctor had said it was fine for her to fly, but cautioned that Kayla's ears may hurt because of the infection she had. Clare had given Kayla her medicine before they boarded the plane, so she would be drowsy and not panic during the flight. Clare smoothed her daughter's short wavy brown hair from her eyes and sat back.

Jim reclined in his chair and closed his eyes. Clare stared out of the window looking down at the world from up in the sky. There was so much you don't see from the ground, like the outlines of the houses, fields, rivers, and the different shapes the clouds made. Everything was magnificent from up here. It had to be God's gift. Who else, or what else for that matter, could make something so beautiful and extraordinary?

Clare once dreamed about flying in the sky. She thought that if she came back after she died, through reincarnation, she wanted to be a bird. That way she could see how beautiful the world is, and everything that God had made for us to enjoy.

She closed her eyes and wondered if what she thought was normal. Thinking about her relationship with Jim and how it used to be when they first met, she remembered it wasn't this chaotic. There had been nothing but love between them, but now she couldn't even look at him like she once did. When she used to wake up in the morning, she'd slide up against him and feel the warmth of his body. They'd make passionate love over and over until their bodies expended what little energy they had left. They'd gaze into each other's eyes as Clare stroked his face. Of course, they didn't have Kayla yet, but their old life shouldn't have changed the way they felt about each other. Many people have children and they still embrace each other with love, so what happened to them—what happened to Jim?

Ever since he lost his supervisor position at the factory where they both worked together and was given an hourly job, he'd become violent. Clare wondered what she did to make him act this way. These days she thought twice before saying anything to him. The wrong words would set him off, but it only seemed to happen when he was drinking. When he was sober, he acted as if the world was a beautiful place and no wrong ever happened.

Two hours later, the flight attendant announced that they would be landing. Kayla was sitting up, eager to get out of her seat and run around the plane. Jim opened his eyes and smiled at Clare. She smiled back. Moments like these gave her such hope that he'd get better and not hurt them anymore.

As Clare helped to gather the luggage, Kayla shouted from her stroller, "Grammy is here! Grammy is here!" Clare turned in the direction Kayla was pointing and waved when she saw Grammy who looked much younger than she'd remembered. Her hair was cut into a bob and dyed red.

Clare was surprised by how much weight Grammy had lost since she'd moved to Florida. Papa Benny stood next to her and he reminded Clare of George Carlin, the comedian, with his similar face and white hair.

Clare gave her mother-in-law and Papa Benny a hug. Within half an hour, they were entering the community where they lived. Clare stared through the window and watched the palm trees sway in the breeze. The bright blue sky was inviting, and the warm sun beamed down from above. She loved this place. It was so beautiful and

14

breathtaking. She'd been to Florida many times as a child going to Disney World, but never this far south.

Here in Naples, the smell of salt water met her senses as she inhaled; it was paradise. The beauty of the palms and warmth that surrounded her took away all her worries and fears; and she felt as if all the pain of the past had disappeared.

****

Several hours after climbing into bed, Clare jolted awake when she heard the screams coming from her daughter's room. She rushed to her bed to hold her until she calmed down. After she gave Kayla her medicine, she lay down with her and stroked her hair as they both drifted off to sleep.

****

The morning sun shone on Clare's face, waking her as she slept on the foldout bed in the family room. Trying not to wake Kayla, she slid out from under the blankets and made her way onto the lanai where she could see the birds flying from tree to tree. At only 6:30 a.m., the sun was already making the air hot around her.

Their condo sat near a golf course. From her perch, Clare could see the workers begin mowing the grass and raking the sand pits for the golfers. She couldn't understand the concept of hitting the ball, driving, or walking to where it landed, then hitting the ball again until it dropped into the hole.

The number of people who were up at this hour surprised her. Some were walking the path along the outer perimeter of the condominiums and some were jogging or riding their bikes.

A slight breeze tousled her hair and she closed her eyes, taking in the warm air. She hadn't felt this relaxed in a long time. The sound of the glass slider rolling on its track startled Clare as Jim joined her outside. He pulled her into his arms and kissed her cheek. Clare felt butterflies in her stomach as he embraced her. They hadn't held each other like this in so long, and it felt wonderful.

"It would be so great to live here, don't you think?" Jim asked.

"Yes, it would. I could get used to waking up and feeling the warmth on my face and seeing blue skies every day. It sure would be different from Ohio."

"So, what's stopping us from doing it? Let's move. I know my mom would love to have us here, and enjoy seeing her granddaughter whenever she wanted.

"We need to tie up loose ends in Ohio, first and remember, we have to go to court. My family is there and your sister's, too. We need jobs, a place to live in, and we have Kayla to worry about."

"Just a thought," Jim huffed. He released Clare and lit a cigarette. Clare stared out at the sky. *It would be nice to live here*, she thought.

She decided to look in the newspaper for jobs in medical claims and billing. The medical business was much better down here than up north and paid more per hour. Clare found fourteen contacts to send her resume to when she returned home. She folded the newspaper and slipped it into her purse.

They spent most of the day at the beach with Kayla playing in the sand and splashing in the water. As Clare sat on the beach watching Jim and Kayla build a sandcastle, she thought about moving down here and how much better their life might be. Jim seemed to be spending more time with them and becoming more affectionate toward Clare. He didn't often play with Kayla at home. Maybe all her prayers were being answered and moving down to Florida is what they needed.

Returning to Grammy's condominium, Clare realized she'd spent way too much time in the sun. Clare didn't put as much lotion on as she did with Kayla, so her skin had burned and was tender to the touch. Jim was smart to bring a T-shirt with him, but he was more brown than red.

****

The week flew by and before they knew it, they were preparing to head back. Clare was surprised Papa Benny had stayed sober while they were visiting. He usually hated having company, as he was more of a loner. Grammy often told Clare what he would say to her, that he wanted a divorce or for her to get out. Then during the next day or two he'd apologize and swear he didn't mean it.

Papa Benny, a hard-working businessman, could be sweet and caring when he wanted, especially when he wasn't drinking. He and Grammy had moved here a few years ago. It was the one place he wanted to live, but he knew he'd have to obtain a transfer from his job to do so. They both worked in nursing facilities as managers handling finances and the other responsibilities of the facility while living in the building they managed. Papa Benny wanted to move to Florida where it was warm, but he knew Grammy would have a difficult time leaving her kids who were all grown up, to move fourteen hundred miles away, but she did, and she had no regrets. At least that's what she told Clare.

Clare could tell that Papa Benny loved Grammy and would do anything for her, just as she loved and cared for him.

Jim and Clare said their goodbyes and went through security. Clare gave Kayla her medicine before they boarded the plane, hoping it would alleviate the pain in her ears. The flight home was exhausting, but Clare couldn't get the thought of moving to Florida out of her head.

She spent the next couple of days revamping her resume and faxing it. By the end of the week, she had sent fourteen faxes and received six responses. When she wrote the cover letter, she made it clear that they would be moving down in February.

The other eight weren't too happy about waiting, but Clare was ecstatic about the new adventure ahead.

****

Jim decided to quit his job two weeks after they got back and talked Clare into doing the same, but she wanted to wait until after going to court for the bankruptcy hearing in January before quitting. She took care of the bills and didn't want to fall short on paying them, which happened anyway because neither one could cash their

401Ks until after the court date. So, they asked Jim's dad for money and Clare assured him that he would be paid back as soon as they cashed their checks.

****

Christmas came, and Clare had to tell her family that they were moving to Florida. If they were unhappy, they didn't show it.

January arrived and they went to court. The bankruptcy went through, and they cashed their checks, which made Clare feel more at ease. She had paid all the bills in advance and repaid Jim's father.

They were moving to Florida. Everything that had happened in the last two years seemed like a blur. They'd lost everything—at least everything that meant something to Clare.

She sorted through the photos she'd taken of their first house together, the house that wasn't theirs any longer. They had lived with Clare's parents for a year while their house was being built. Clare had bought a six-and-a-half-acre wooded lot and had a dome house with three bedrooms and two full baths built on it. When they were able to move in, she painted all the rooms herself and did all the decorating.

Wiping away her tears, she stuffed the pictures back into their envelope, piled more books in the box, and then sealed the box. All she remembered now was how hard she'd worked to build that house. Jim didn't have any money set aside when they met, but Clare had sold another piece of land she'd bought as well as her first car. She was the one who was paying for everything and the money was soon gone.

They'd moved three times, but she couldn't wait to move out of this townhouse. It was next door to a girl from work who she didn't get along with at work. She didn't know why the girl didn't like her, but Clare surely didn't like her sister who lived there as well. The sister whom Jim tried to have sex with one night, yet he claimed she came on to him, kissing him and touching him; which was enough to make Clare nauseated when he told her. Clare wanted to believe him, but these past two years made it hard to believe anything he said.

She finished packing in two days, though most of their belongings were in a storage unit when they moved out of the house. In four days, they were renting the moving truck and driving south to Florida.

Zeya Culback, Jim's sister, would be riding with him in the truck. Zeya hadn't seen her mom in almost a year because of a lack of money.

Grammy thought it was a wonderful idea and was thrilled with her coming to visit. Besides, Jim could use the company since Clare would be driving down in her car with Kayla.

****

Before going to see her parents, Clare drove to her friend Angel's house, but she knew it would be hard to say goodbye to her friend of ten years. Angel was always there for Clare to lean on when things went wrong in her life.

After pulling into the driveway, Clare parked the car and got out. Angel stood on the porch with her arms crossed in front of her. Her long blonde hair was pulled back into a ponytail. Clare couldn't remember the last time she wore it that way.

"Hi, Angel," Clare greeted her, choking back her tears. Angel opened her arms and embraced her.

"I'm going to miss you, you know. Who am I going to lean on when you're gone?" Angel asked.

"I'm going to miss you too. I wish you could come with me," Clare whispered. "I'm just a phone call away.

We'll keep in touch. I promise." They held each other and cried.

"I promise too, but you're right, we'll keep in touch."

After saying their goodbyes, Clare wiped the tears streaming down her cheeks and drove away. She wasn't sure how she'd manage without Angel, but she had to learn and hold her own.

More tears surfaced when Clare hugged her mom. Saying goodbye was the hardest thing, she had to do.

"You don't have to go, you know," Clare's mom whispered in her ear, which made Clare cry harder. *But she knew she should go, she wanted to go, although Jim's moods and the process of moving were more overwhelming than she'd anticipated. Something inside told her that everything would work out in the end. At least that's what she'd told herself. How could it get any worse than what had happened already?*

Two

Clare

The drive down didn't take as long as Clare had predicted. They made stops to eat, filled up the gas tank, and took one night to sleep. Kayla enjoyed the ride, but she mostly slept or watched a movie on the DVD player that Clare bought for her before they left.

They arrived within two days and unloaded their belongings into a storage unit, until they were able to find a place to live. In the meantime, they'd be staying with Grammy and Papa Benny.

****

The following morning, Clare arranged for an interview at Naples Immediate Care and was meeting the Vice President in two hours. Clare sat waiting for Wendy Burr, the Vice President of the Clinic. The interview didn't take more than an hour, and Clare was eager to start her new job on Monday. She'd be working the front desk with two other people. As she took in a deep breath, the tension rolled off her shoulders.

Arriving back at the condominium, she joined Jim and his mom on the lanai.

"How did it go?" asked Jim.

"I got the job. I start out at a better wage per hour than I was earning in Ohio."

"That's wonderful," Grammy said. "When do you start?"

"I start on Monday, which will give us time to find a place."

"I have some great news too, Clare," Jim interrupted. "I got a job as an electrician with Cable and Sons."

"That's awesome." Clare wrapped her arms around him and kissed his lips. "Now we just have to find a home."

"That's the other good news. I have three condominiums set up for us to look at when you're ready. Mom said she'd watch Kayla."

Clare hoped that things were falling into place. Maybe it wasn't a bad idea after all to move down here. The sun was shining, and it was nearing eighty degrees at a little past 11:00 a.m.

"I'm ready now if you want to go," Clare replied.

The first condominium was in the same vicinity as Grammy's apartment, but a couple of driveways down and a different owner rented it. A two-bedroom condo on the third floor, it had a kitchen, living room and a small laundry area. It wasn't the cleanest place Clare had seen, and for the price, it wasn't big enough either, but of course, they weren't in the north anymore.

The second place was farther away and much smaller than the last, and the cost was still more than Clare wanted to pay. The walls needed paint, and it had an odor. She rubbed her belly trying to calm the nausea. The floors creaked, and the carpet had soil marks. Clare finished walking through and stood outside to get some fresh air.

There was no way in hell she was going to live in a place like that. They may not be rich, but they certainly weren't poor, and she had to think of Kayla.

The third condominium was somewhat bigger but located twenty miles from the beach, so the cost was cheaper. The rooms were wider, and it was on the first floor. Clare saw a short, medium built man standing in the parking lot. Her eyes focused on his hair. It was light brown, and she could tell it was a toupee. She snickered to herself, thinking about the wind blowing it off his head.

26

As you walked through the front door of the apartment there was a long hallway and to the left was a small bedroom with a huge bay window. Next to the bedroom was a stackable washer and dryer hidden away inside a small closet, and beside it was a full-size bathroom that was decorated with pink and yellow flowered wallpaper. *Very outdated*, Clare thought. *Don't these people ever redo the condominiums they own?*

The kitchen area was across the hall from the first small bedroom. It didn't look any bigger than the full-sized bathroom and no more than one person could stand in it at a time. There was a ledge on the kitchen counter, like a bar. The living room space was narrow instead of wide and had a balcony at the end. She walked through the living room, opened the slider to the outside, and imagined waking up and sitting outside drinking her coffee. The balcony was screened in, so bugs and geckos couldn't come in. Entering the condominium again, she went into the master bedroom and saw another closet and a full-size bathroom off to the left.

The hallway, bathrooms, and kitchen were the only rooms with tiles on the floors. The bedrooms and living room had carpet.

Satisfied with what she'd seen, she walked back into the hallway where Jim and the owner Ken Watts were standing. Clare knew that this was the place. She pulled Jim aside and they discussed the terms.

"We'll take it," Jim said to Ken. "How much do we need to put down to move in?"

"First and last month's rent with five hundred security," Ken replied.

"When can we move in?" Clare asked.

"This weekend if you like, say Friday."

Clare made out the checks and handed them to Ken. "Thank you for your time today, we appreciate your showing us the condo," Clare said.

"No, thank you. Condos around here go quick, so you have to grab them while you can," said Ken as he reached into his briefcase and handed Clare a copy of the community agreement. "Rent is due the first of every month and the address is on the papers I just gave you. Once the papers are signed, the place is all yours. Make sure you read them, for they are fussy about the rules around here. It's two parking spaces per condo and the rest are visitors' parking. There is a pool on the other side of the community, and you will need this key to open the gate to access it." He handed the key to Jim. "If you have any questions, my number is on the paper. Feel free to call if you need anything."

"Thanks, Ken." Clare looked through the papers and then around the room.

Finishing the paperwork, they all walked out and said their goodbyes. The drive back to Grammy's house was quiet as Clare daydreamed about furnishing their new home. She stared out of the window at all the homes and shops they passed wondering why she hadn't noticed them earlier.

****

The week went by fast as Friday approached and they packed all their things in a rented moving truck and started organizing their new condominium. Clare did most of the unpacking, while Jim brought in the boxes. By that night, they had completed everything.

They spent Saturday shopping for groceries and a set of furniture to put on their outdoor area. That evening, Kayla played in her room while Clare made dinner. For the first time in a long while, she felt like they were a family again.

****

Rolling over, Clare pressed the button on the alarm as it buzzed. She couldn't believe how the weekend had flown by and today she was starting her new job. Zeya said she'd watch Kayla while they went to work. Clare spent time going through the Yellow Pages to look for a daycare where she could register Kayla in and found one a mile away. She planned on stopping in after work to check the place out and perhaps signing up Kayla. Zeya had talked to Clare last week about living down here permanently. She said she would watch Kayla for them, and they could just pay her the money instead of a daycare, but she wasn't sure if she could stay.

****

After parking her car, Clare strolled into the Immediate Care building. She introduced herself, and got comfortable in a chair at the front counter where she'd be working. David, a guy that had been there for over three years, showed her what she'd be doing. His brunette hair hung over his eyes as he explained the job to her.

Her heart raced, as she started to feel overwhelmed by the amount of people stampeding through the front doors. She greeted the first patient and took her insurance card, then entered the information while the woman filled out paperwork. She was being treated for a cough that she'd had for over two weeks. Clare heard a baby cry in the lobby to the right who was being treated for excessive vomiting.

Clare wasn't the only one working at the front desk. Along with David, there was Cathy, who had been there for several months.

It was 3:00 p.m. when she looked at the clock on the wall behind her. She filed patient folders in a rollaway cabinet for the last two hours before leaving. Organizing was one of Clare's best talents and it passed the time when there was no work at the front desk to do.

After finishing up, she went over to the time clock and punched out for the day. On the drive home the traffic was unbelievable. There were vehicles lined up for miles. Clare didn't care for traffic nor was she used to it, after having lived in the country. She drove to the daycare near their condominium and talked to an elderly woman running the facility. They were taking registrations that week, which Clare was thankful for, and she signed Kayla up after the tour. She wrote a check and headed home to see her daughter.

"Yea, Mommy's home from work," Kayla shouted as she ran down the hall into Clare's arms.

"Yes, sweetheart, Mommy's home!"

Clare talked to Zeya about the daycare and then said their goodbyes. She watched Kayla from the kitchen while she made dinner. Jim arrived at 6:15p.m. and gave them both kisses before he went to have a shower.

During the meal, they spent time discussing their day. Jim was exhausted and mentioned how hot it was working outdoors, but nothing more. He asked Clare to fill up the water cooler for him tomorrow, so he didn't get dehydrated. She nodded, finished her meal, and then started washing the dishes.

That night they made love for the first time since they'd moved and fell asleep in each other's arms.

The following morning, Clare took Kayla to the daycare and walked her in. After showing her around, she kissed her on the cheek and hugged her goodbye.

****

Weeks passed by, and Clare was flying around the office. She had always been a fast learner, and this job was so much easier on her physically since she'd quit the factory where she'd worked up north. She had worked at the plant for ten years. Cabinet Makers, Inc. was one of the best jobs anyone could have in Ohio, since 9/11. Most of the other factories had closed down when the Twin Towers were hit. People were lucky to have any job around the world. The work she did, abused her arms, and she was diagnosed with carpal tunnel syndrome, but she took the money from the case instead of having the surgery because they had moved to Florida. The abdominal pain she'd been experiencing went away, probably because of having a hysterectomy last year, and her relationship with Jim was better than it had been in a long time.

Three

Jim Culback

Jim reached for the wall, propped himself up and then vomited everywhere. He'd been working in the heat for days and his body was feeling the effect. No matter how much water he drank, it was never enough. He'd already gone through the water cooler in the morning and he had another four hours to go. Feeling dizzy, he held onto the wall while throwing up once more. Juan Garcia, who'd been working with Jim since he started, poked his head around the corner to check on him.

"You don't look so good, Jim. Maybe you should get out of the heat and cool down," Juan advised.

Jim ran a hand through his short dark hair, wiped his mouth, then headed over to the company van. He hadn't been feeling good for a while, but he didn't want to tell Juan or Clare. He knew it was from the heat, but if he couldn't handle it, then what was he going to do? He thought it was better not to say a word to either of them. Clare had seemed so relaxed and happy since they'd come down to the area, so he didn't want to burst her bubble if he didn't feel the same.

Sitting in the van with the air conditioning running, he began to feel better. Thinking of the past couple weeks, Jim lay down and closed his eyes. *How can I tell her that I hate my job? That feeling this way makes me unhappy and going to a job that I really don't like makes me want to drink again. I know she won't like it if I do. She won't understand that I need it, but I need a drink—I need to relax and be myself. My head feels like it wants to explode.* His body quivered at the thought of having a drink. *One drink, that's all I want. She won't know if I have one. I'll cover the smell, yes, that's what I'll do.* Jim sat up and smiled. The queasiness had subsided, but the thoughts of drinking remained. Jim got out of the van and headed back to work in a happier spirit.

"Do you want to come over and have a drink with me after work?" Juan offered. "On Fridays a few of my friends come over and we just sit around and talk. Just let me know and I'll give you my address."

"Sounds good, but I'll have to get back to you. Got to talk to my wife about it first," Jim replied. He didn't have to talk to Clare about going because he knew she would freak out again.

"Sure, no problem. That's one thing I don't have to worry about. I've never been married. I guess I haven't found the right one."

"Marriage isn't that bad, but I do miss doing my own thing when I want." Jim reached for the electrical box and connected the wires together. One more box to set up and they were done with this job and then off until the next one on Monday.

Jim was relieved. It had been a long week and this heat was enough to make anyone sick. Overall, Jim didn't actually hate his job; it was more the heat than anything.

Jim finished up, collected his tools, and put them back into the van. He dug in his jeans' pocket and fished out his cell phone to call Clare but got her voicemail. He left her a message stating he was going over to Juan Garcia's house and chill for a while and then maybe do some fishing, and that he'd talk to her later. After hanging up, he was glad that she hadn't answered her phone. Jim drove the van back to the warehouse and began putting the tools in his jeep.

"I'll follow you to your house," Jim yelled to Juan who was walking to his car.

"Sounds good. See you there."

Jim started his jeep and followed. His stereo was jamming so loud that the speakers were vibrating the metal. It was a birthday present from Clare even though he had to beg a little. He always got what he wanted, even if it took some begging; she'd always give into him, kind of like twisting someone's arm until they gave in. It sounded selfish, but that's who he was now. She didn't like his actions, and that's why he drank, to feel good about himself. Clare always called him an asshole when he drank, but she just didn't get who he was.

Jim turned the stereo louder to block out the thoughts entering his head. He hated thinking, but it was hard to stop his mind from what it wanted to do. Drinking stopped the mind, well; at least that's what Jim kept telling himself.

Jim passed the road that connected with their condo and turned at the next light on his way to Juan's house. Pulling into the drive, he parked behind Juan's dark blue Pontiac GT, turned down the stereo, and reached for his phone. He flipped it open and saw a voicemail from Clare, but he hesitated before playing the message.

She was cool with me going to Juan Garcia's house, even though I told her we were going fishing. She has no clue I will be drinking and if I get too drunk, I'll just stay here for the night, he thought.

37

Exiting his vehicle, he glanced around. The outside of the house was covered in moss and vines from the ground to the roof. The front patio was enclosed with a screen, he assumed to keep out the mosquitoes and other vermin. If the house had paint on it, he couldn't tell by the looks of it. At a guess, Jim would say that the house was at least thirty to forty years old.

Entering the house, they passed through the living room. Jim didn't see much furniture, just a couple of leather recliner chairs that were dirty and ripped, and there was a coffee table in front of them. Jim entered the kitchen as Juan opened the refrigerator and grabbed two beers, he then handed one to Jim.

"Here's to a long, hot week at work," Juan said. They clinked bottles and headed to the rear of the house to sit in another enclosed porch.

Jim pressed his lips around the top of the bottle; hesitating a moment before he took a swig; the taste was wet and satisfying, he closed his eyes, chugged down half the bottle, and then decided to finish it. Juan looked surprised, shrugged his shoulders, and pointed to the kitchen, letting Jim know to help himself to another beer.

Jim headed inside. "You have a nice house here, Juan. It seems secluded in these woods," Jim yelled from the kitchen. He grabbed a beer and went back outside.

"Thanks. My mom left it to me when she passed away five years ago. It beats paying rent. The property tax is still high, but I manage."

"Where do you go fishing? What kind of fish do you catch?"

"My friends and I usually hit the lake we found on Bayer Drive. There aren't any bass or walleye down here in Florida, at least not this far south. Mostly sheep-head and crawfish and tons of catfish, but if you go to the Gulf, you will catch sharks and other exotic varieties. The guys will be here soon. If you want, we can take you over to the lake and do some night fishing."

"Sure, that sounds like fun. I used to fish up in Ohio, but not as much as I went hunting. Do you guys do any hunting here?"

"No, you have to go to a class here for gun safety, not something I want to do."

Jim chugged down the rest of his second beer and tapped Juan's to see if he was ready for another. Nodding, Jim slipped into the kitchen and fetched two more,

39

handing one to Juan as he sat back down. They drank quietly on the patio when a knock on the door broke the silence. Juan excused himself and left to answer it.

Jim stood up, stretched, and stared out into the back yard. Birds flew from one tree to the next, singing their songs while geckos slipped through the crack at the bottom of the screen door. Jim heard Juan talking to someone, so he headed out in the yard and lit a cigarette. He continued to enjoy the view until Juan came back out to join him.

"Sorry, that was my neighbor asking if I'd watch his house while he's gone for the weekend."

"That's fine, I was just checking out your backyard." Chugging down his third beer, he nudged Juan to see if he wanted another one. Jim opened the door and made his way to the kitchen. There were only four beers left. He grabbed all four and set two on the kitchen counter. "I'm going to use your bathroom," Jim yelled over his shoulder.

He didn't see any pictures of family hanging on the wall as he trudged down the dreary hallway. Peeking through the first door he came to, he saw a cabinet with several hunting guns. For someone who didn't go hunting, Juan surely had quite a few guns.

Jim pushed open the door and moved closer to get a better look. He knew his guns and noticed a couple of older ones, a .20-gauge shotgun, and two pistols. Off to his right, sitting on the nightstand, was a .357 Magnum. He picked up the gun and glanced at it before putting it back down. He'd asked Clare for a gun like this one, but after his attempted suicide once when he was drunk, she'd said no.

He had a 9mm that her father had helped him buy, but she had taken it away when he was passed out on the living room sofa.

It was one of the many nights he'd called her at work and told her boss that she needed to come home right away. He wasn't sure what time she had returned home, but when he woke the following afternoon, the gun was gone. He knew she had got rid of it and her dad had sold it.

With two beers in hand, he cracked one open and chugged it all, and then set down the empty on the nightstand and picked up the next.

He turned and hurried through the door and back down the hall. The next door was the bathroom. Jim stumbled inside and straddled the toilet with one hand on the wall, he chugged half the bottle not wanting to lose the buzz he was feeling and had waited so long for. He knew he wouldn't be going home tonight, there was no way Clare was going to see him this way. He stood and guzzled the rest of the beer, then made his way back to the kitchen and took the two beers he'd left on the counter and went outside.

"Hey, Jim. Thought you'd got lost in there."

"Yeah, sorry it took so long. Was just admiring your photos on the wall."

"You're funny. I don't like all that clutter on my walls and besides, the rest of my family was killed in Cuba a few years ago by a hurricane."

"Sorry to hear that. Are your friends on their way? We're out of beer, maybe they can stop and get some for us."

"I'll give them a buzz." Juan disappeared into the house to use the phone.

Jim reached in his pocket to retrieve his cell phone and noticed that Clare had called again after he'd shut off the ringer. After listening to the message, he erased it and called her back. After several rings later, she answered.

"Hey, didn't think you were going to call me back."

"Sorry, I was busy with Juan. He went in to call his buddies to see how long they'd be."

"What time do you think you'll be home tonight?"

"I don't know we're going night fishing, so we'll probably be out late. If it's too late, I'll just crash here. Is that okay with you?"

"That's fine. I guess Kayla and I will have a girl's night tonight then. Maybe I'll take her to the park for a while."

"That sounds great. You both have fun, and I'll talk to you later," Jim responded as he swigged down his beer.

"All right, I'll see you when you get home."

"Okay, see you later," he replied, trying not to slur his words.

He pressed the off button and slid the phone back into his pocket.

Four

Detective Parks- Florida

Taking his suitcase from the overhead compartment, Detective Terry Parks coasted down the aisle and then stepped off the plane. Once inside the airport, he stopped at the restroom to freshen up before making his way outside. The intercom made a loud piercing sound as a woman began to speak, "Welcome to Ft. Myers, Florida. The time is now 5:30 p.m. and the temperature is eighty-seven degrees. I hope you had a good flight. Please fly with us again soon, and have a wonderful day."

The sliders opened, and hot air blew across his face. He squinted at the glare of the sun that made its way across the horizon. He reached into his shirt pocket, pulled out a pack of Newport lights, and struck one up.

He'd always enjoyed coming to Florida. The skies were always such a vibrant blue, and the sun was warming to the skin. He needed to get out of the cold weather they were having in Chicago. Just last week they were hit with two feet of snow, and it didn't seem like it was going to stop.

He watched as several people rolled their luggage out to the curb waiting for their ride. A blonde-haired boy tugged on his mom's pant leg and then stretched his arms out wide as she picked him up.

Glancing at his cell phone, he dialed a number. Ten minutes later, a car pulled up, and he got in.

"Hi, Mom. Hi, Dad. Thanks for picking me up." The conversation down to Naples centered on the weather and work. Detective Parks didn't like talking about work with his father because he would get upset that Terry had decided to take a different career path and not work in the family business. He'd always wanted to be a detective, and though the hours were long, it beat sitting at home. It's not like he had a wife or kids to hang out with. It was just him and his dog, Sugarcane who was a gray, black, and brown Husky.

Combing his hand through his thick black hair, though it was getting grayer by the minute, he glanced out of the window trying to block out his father. He just kept rambling on and on about the business, he'd started, and that Terry should not have become a detective. He thought to himself that maybe he should have gone somewhere else for his two-week vacation; he wanted to relax, not listen to the same old complaints over and over. There was more to life than the family business.

He couldn't understand why his dad didn't find a hobby to keep his mind busy instead of dwelling on what he couldn't change. It wasn't like the printing business would take over the world.

Pulling into the driveway, Detective Parks flung his coat over his arm and climbed out. This was the first time in a year that he'd been at the house since they had it repainted.

"The house looks great, Mom. It really brings out the features in the stone they used when the house was built."

"Thanks. I think it looks great too. You have to see the new colors in the kitchen and dining room when you come into the house," his mom said. She'd always wanted to repaint the inside of the house, ever since they bought it five years ago.

The kitchen had a lemon-yellow hue, but he couldn't tell the difference until the lights were on. In the dining area, where one of the round glass tables sat, the wall was now painted an olive green to break up the space of the room.

Opening the door to the elevator off the kitchen area, he climbed inside with his suitcase and rode to the second floor. Entering the guest bedroom, he placed his suitcase on the daybed that was against the wall to his right. The slider doors connected one wall to the other, and in the winter months, he loved to open them up and let in the cool air. Beyond the sliders was a tiled outdoor enclosure that covered the back of the house. At night, he'd sit out there and relax, just soaking in the night air.

After changing into shorts, he joined his parent's downstairs. They decided to go out to eat, since it was past 6:00 p.m. and his mom didn't feel like cooking. They chose Joe's Crab Shack for dinner because the family was big on seafood.

It was past 9:00 p.m. when they got back to the house. Detective Parks stayed up for a while longer watching television with his parents and then retired to his room upstairs.

He lay in bed reflecting on the conversation his dad began at dinner. His mom didn't say a word as his father drilled him on when he would find a woman to settle down with and get married.

"You're thirty-five years old and still not married. What is wrong with you, Terry?"

He replied as he always did, "Just waiting on the right woman to come along, that's all."

It bothered him when his dad got onto him. What was the rush anyway? He was healthy, and supported himself. Besides, most of the women he had dated didn't care for the long hours he worked, so he'd rather not date. His dad was right though as he did want to get married one day, but he just hadn't found the right one. He had faith that it would happen when he least expected it. There was too much going on at work to date someone now anyway.

Just last week, he, and his partner finally cracked a case from seven months ago. They thought for sure that the missing boy was dead. There had been other young boys that didn't live long after they were kidnapped, but this case had missing parts and it was like someone purposely didn't collect all the evidence. He couldn't believe that the person they arrested was capable of murder; he seemed like a good person and was well respected.

Kidnapping the boys, raped them, and then disposed their bodies in the canal on Michigan Avenue, shocked the community. What puzzled Parks the most was that he kept the last boy longer, so they weren't sure why he was any different than the previous seven the man had killed.

Detective Parks went undercover for four months before finally linking the Catholic priest as the one responsible. He had been a long-time friend of the family; someone they didn't think could harm a child, and who the community trusted.

Parks was out on his morning run before dawn the day he cracked the case, and just like every morning, he'd jog past the Catholic Church. He wasn't certain what he saw that morning, but it bothered him enough to request a meeting with his captain when he went into work. He should have figured the case out earlier because all the missing boys were local and troubled children who belonged to the church.

He was just relieved that the case was solved, and the priest was behind bars for good, but after just one week in prison, the priest was stabbed to death in his jail cell. *That's one creep off the streets,* Terry thought before closing his eyes and going to sleep.

****

The next morning, Parks and his dad spent time fishing and took out the new boat that his dad had purchased. His dad scared him when he whipped into the bay too fast and almost took out the dock. The guy's pushing eighty. He shouldn't be trying to drive a boat ten times the size of his Cadillac, especially if he's afraid of it.

****

Before he knew it, the two weeks had passed by and he was flying back home. His cell phone rang as he entered the front door of his home, but he let it go to voicemail. It was his father calling again and he didn't want to get into the same conversation they'd been having the last two weeks with him. Before he left Florida, his father once again was on his case about being a detective and unmarried. He was tired of hearing about being single.

He set his bags down, took a bottle of water from the refrigerator, then walked to the pool house to check the water level. He recently had the pool house built, so he could swim in the winter months and all year round if he wanted to. There were days he'd do fifty to sixty laps in the pool and then work out in the gym he had in the basement. He was five feet, eleven inches tall and weighed one hundred and eighty pounds. When the doctor had told him he would become diabetic if he didn't lose the weight, he went on a diet and started working out. As a result, he was now ninety pounds lighter. Besides working on crime, he'd keep himself busy by staying in shape.

Walking back through the tunnel he had attached from the house to the pool, he strolled through the finished basement and checked out his Beatle collection before heading upstairs to go and retrieve Sugarcane from the vet. The vet closed at 3:00 p.m. in the afternoon.

Glancing at the clock on the wall, he saw he had an hour to get there, when it would only take him fifteen minutes.

****

That evening, he turned on the news and listened to the latest crimes. He wished he could make the violence stop, but then he wouldn't have the work he did; he relished helping to fix some of the world's problems. After turning off the television off, he sat down in his office and checked his messages.

The first one was his good partner Detective Gary Brown calling and welcoming him home, adding that he needed to talk to him about a case. The second and last message was his father calling him and wanting him to call when he was settled in at home. After deleting the messages, he hesitated before dialing his father.

51

Five

Clare

Clare didn't want to believe he was drinking again. She hoped he wouldn't start again after leaving Ohio, but she'd heard him slur his words and that was enough for her to believe it. Her hands wouldn't stop trembling as she set down the phone. Kayla was playing in her room when Clare came in.

"Hey, sweetie." She swallowed. "Do you want to go to the park?" She hoped going to the park would take her mind off Jim.

Kayla squealed with joy and jumped to her feet. "Yes, yes, yes, I do, Mommy." She hurried to put her sandals on and ran into her mom's arms. Clare took her purse from the counter, and they headed out the door.

She tried several times to call Jim, but she kept getting his voicemail. Kayla played on the monkey bars, and then made her way to the swings, her brown wavy hair bouncing as she skipped and jumped on the seat. "Push me, Momma!" she yelled. "Push me really fast."

Clare didn't feel like leaving him a message, so she stuck the phone in her back pocket and focused on her daughter. She knew what he was doing when he was out. She really wanted to be wrong, but she could feel in her gut that she wasn't.

****

After the park, they stopped for a bite to eat and took some pictures at a resort near their apartment. The horses looked real, but were made of brass or steel. A man and his family were also looking at the horses and offered to take pictures of them. There were six galloping horses, and flowers in a variety of colors making different designs. They spelled, *Lely Resorts*, in red, yellow, and white mums.

After they had finished taking pictures, Clare thanked the family and headed for home. It was past 9:00 p.m. when they got back, but she knew Jim wouldn't be there, so she locked the door behind her and took Kayla to the bathroom to get washed up and ready for bed.

Clare made her way to the bedroom, stopping off in the kitchen to take the phone off the hook; she knew if he was drinking that he would be calling her later. He always called her asking for her to collect him because he was too drunk to drive. Picking him up instead of him driving wasn't a bad thing, but then she had to put Kayla in the car and go get him. She hated when he would beg her to pick him up. He was so obnoxious and would swear at her for no reason. If Clare even tried to tell him to shut his mouth, he'd cut her down, and tell her how worthless she was and that she should mind her own fucking business. She hated his foul mouth when he was drunk, especially around Kayla.

She reached for her cell phone and crept out onto the balcony. By the time she went back in, it was past 11:00 p.m. She changed her clothes, crawled under the covers, and shut the phone off before falling asleep.

****

The sun brightened the room when she forced her eyes open and glanced at the alarm clock. It was 6:00 a.m. in the morning and no Jim beside her. Sitting up, she reached for her cell and turned it on. She slid out of bed and went to the bathroom waiting for her phone to come alive. When she had finished, she grabbed the phone and headed outside.

There were two messages on her phone. She listened to the first one, but wasn't sure if she understood, so she replayed it. "You have got to be kidding me," she mumbled as her heart quickened. She played the message once more to be sure she heard it correctly. The second message was blank, so she hit delete and went inside to write down the number the woman on the phone had left her.

Clare didn't know what to do, it was excessively early to call anyone, but she knew she should try the number hoping that the woman was still working. After getting the run around, she was finally transferred to someone who explained what to do and where to go.

Clare looked at the clock, knowing that she had to be at work by 10:00 a.m. that morning. The Immediate Care scheduled her to work every other weekend. It was now 7:15 a.m., and she needed someone to watch Kayla for the day. She didn't want to wake Grammy up, but what other choice did she have, considering the predicament she was in? Zeya answered the phone.

Clare told her that Jim never came home last night and what time she had to be at work.

"What happened last night, Clare?" Zeya asked.

Clare filled her in on what she knew and told her about the message she'd received around 3:30 a.m. in the morning.

"He's in jail?"

"I'm afraid so. I guess he had tried to call me collect, but my cell phone doesn't accept collect calls. I don't know what to do. I have to go to work because we need the money, and I've only just started there. I guess I can't go to the jail in Ft. Myers until I get out at 2:00 p.m. I mean, there's nothing I can do right now." Tears slid down her face.

"What the hell is he doing in Ft. Myers?"

"I've asked myself that question too, but I'm sure he has a story behind it. He always has a story to tell."

"If I wasn't leaving later today, I'd chew his ass out. What the hell is wrong with my brother?"

"If you ever figure him out, please let me know. Thank you, Zeya, for listening to me ramble on. I'll be there within an hour, and we'll talk about what I need to do later." After hanging up the phone, Clare woke Kayla and got ready for work.

Sharp pains bolted through her stomach, which happened every time Jim did something stupid. Gathering the things Kayla would need for the day, she rushed out of the door. She would have to go to the bank on her lunch break to get the money. She didn't know how much it would cost to get him out of jail, so she figured a thousand would have to be enough. She even decided to call the man back that Jim was buying a fishing boat from to tell him that she was canceling the check for the fifteen hundred today. The man had said he understood and to let him know if she needed anything.

Clare kept busy at work. Patients poured into the building as if everyone was sick at the same time, but it was enough to keep Clare's mind off Jim.

****

Driving along unfamiliar streets, she followed the directions that the sheriff gave her on the phone. She found the where the jail was located and parked the car. She entered the building and spoke with the clerk. He advised her to go across the street and post bail, and then he would be released after they had received the paperwork showing that she had paid. He reminded her before leaving that it would take several hours after, for him to be released.

She cut across the street and talked to a man behind the counter.

"Since you haven't lived here for six months, I'll need an extra hundred because you are not a resident of Florida." With no other choice, she paid the five hundred and took the paperwork back to the jail. Now, all she had to do was wait. She knew she couldn't leave her car where it was, so she drove around to find a parking spot. After walking back to the jail, she sat in the lobby and chatted with another girl who was waiting for her boyfriend to be released.

"Let's go for a walk, I think it is going to be quite a while before they get out," Lisa said.

She had blue hair with red streaks and a nose ring; not someone Clare was comfortable around, but she didn't want to walk to a store alone. They found a small convenience store a few blocks from the jail and bought a couple soft drinks and a small bag of chips. She still wasn't feeling hungry but knew she needed to eat.

Hours passed, and Jim still wasn't released. It was 7:00 p.m. and then 8:00 p.m.; the minutes seemed to pass by in slow motion. By 10:00 p.m., Clare was exhausted, so she made her way to her car, which was parked two blocks away.

As she looked around in the dark shadowy parking lot, she shivered from the thought of someone hurting her or something worse. Her car was the only one parked there. A tree branch snapped and fell to the ground. Not thinking twice, she bolted to the car, jumped into the driver's seat and locked the door.

As her eyes searched the darkness, she hoped and prayed that no one was watching her, but were her eyes playing tricks on her, or did she really see someone, or something move by the side of the building? She turned the key and the lights beamed onto the wall, but there was no one there. Her eyes were just over tired. There was nothing out there, she told herself, so she turned on the radio to escape the silence around her. Being alone in the dark and in a town, she wasn't familiar with, made her want to gather up Kayla and go back to Ohio where she felt safe.

She thought about the conversation she had with her sister that morning. Jodi had called her on the way to Grammy's house, saying that Jim called her collect. She didn't want to accept the call, but thought maybe something was wrong with Clare. Jodi told her not to bail his ass out because he needed to learn his lesson. As much as Clare wanted to leave him in jail, she had fears of not being able to survive without him. How would she be able to afford the rent and take care of Kayla? She wouldn't be able to pay for daycare, a place to live in, and all the other necessities that go along with life. There'd be no money left to buy food. Her heart accelerated. She didn't need to have another panic attack, not now.

What the hell was he thinking anyway, driving up here? We had never even been to Ft. Myers before. The sheriff told Clare that she'd pulled him over after he drove out of a parking lot and almost hit another car. The sheriff did a DUI test on him and he failed.

Before Clare had met Jim, he already had five DUIs, though he'd tell you that one was a reckless op. It still didn't make a difference if one of his arrests was a reckless op because he shouldn't have been drinking and driving. He admitted when he was pulled over in Ohio, that he told the cops that he was Jesus; because of the sandals, he was wearing. Clare got a good laugh from that every time. *What a jerk! Why does this have to happen? He was doing so well not drinking, and now he's started up again. Is he ever going to stop drinking? Am I going to have to live like this forever?*

That was something Clare didn't want to do. If she could afford to have a place of her own with Kayla, she'd be gone in a heartbeat. Yes, she loved him, but sometimes love wasn't enough in a relationship—she knew she wanted more than just love with an abuser.

She wanted someone who'd protect her and stand by her on any decision she made, to love her for the woman she was and never cheat on her. It seemed that whomever she got involved with, they were always unfaithful to her. It's not like she didn't have sex with them. It just didn't seem like they got enough from her, or maybe she just wasn't good enough for them; at least that's what she kept telling herself.

Her health wasn't the best in that area, with or without the pain. She had pain during intercourse, but hid it from the guys she dated. After the doctors took out the cancer, she developed endometriosis and sex had been painful ever since, until she had the hysterectomy last year.

Her mind flashed back to a night a few weeks after the surgery. She was woken by loud music, so she trudged outside and found Jim's vehicle in the front yard near their bedroom. She banged on the window of Jim's truck until he rolled it down. One whiff was all it took. He was drunk. He got so pissed at her for telling him to turn down the radio, that he floored the accelerator and spun grass and dirt at Clare. She went back inside to check on Kayla, but the door to her bedroom wouldn't budge. She pushed harder and poked her head in to find Kayla lying on the other side of the door holding her teddy bear. Clare made her way in and lifted Kayla into her arms. She grabbed her stuff and climbed into the car in the garage. She was going to her parents' house.

When Clare opened the garage door, Jim's truck was blocking her in. He ran to her car and reached into the back to get Kayla out. Clare literally jumped from the front to the back, getting Kayla away from him. They argued and went back inside as Clare tried to calm down Kayla who was crying from all the commotion. Jim stomped out of the room, grabbed his 9mm gun, and then left in his truck. Clare took Kayla to the sofa and held her close to her.

Half an hour later, there were blue and red lights flashing as they pulled into her drive. She opened the front door after one of the officers knocked. The officer had told her they received a call from Jim stating he was going to kill himself. She responded back that he wasn't home and had left out of here in a hurry—she didn't actually know where he was. Minutes later, he spun up the drive and bolted into the house. The police cuffed him and said they were taking him to the hospital where he could get help.

It didn't work.

Clare pushed the seat back and lay down. Closing her eyes, she hoped to get some sleep, knowing she had to work in the morning. The time on the radio read 11:30 p.m. and he still wasn't out yet.

Her phone rang and she sprang up to search for it.

"Hello."

"Where are you? I'm standing outside the jail. Can you come get me?" Jim said.

"I'm right down the road. I'll be there in a minute." Starting the car, she drove down the street and saw he was standing with several other men as she approached him. She slowed to a halt, and Jim jumped in the passenger seat and then started crying like a baby.

"I'm never going to drink again," he claimed. "I'm so sorry, Clare, for doing this to you. Get me out of here. I want to go home." Neither one said another word. What was there to say? To her, it would be more broken promises.

It wasn't long before the alarm started to blare, waking Clare from a dead sleep.

Jim lay beneath the blanket still sleeping as Clare padded to the kitchen to make coffee. Last night seemed like a dream when she woke that morning, but she knew it was far from that. She had never experienced anything like last night. It was the first time she had to bail him out of jail, and now with court coming up and the fines to pay she would have to work more hours. They even towed his jeep and would have to find the impound lot on Monday; thank goodness she didn't have to work that day. They took his driver's license from him, so she wasn't sure if he'd be driving the jeep back.

Clare woke Jim up before leaving for work and told him that his mom would be dropping off Kayla in a couple of hours. Picking up his clothes from the night before, she removed his wallet and threw the bundle in the washer. She hated the smell of smoke and beer on his clothes when he had been out drinking.

Standing in the kitchen, she searched his wallet to see how much money he'd spent. Her heart sank when she found his wedding band stuffed in with the money he had left. Pain stabbed at her heart as if someone was pricking it with a knife. *How could he do this to me again? What am I doing wrong? Do I not love him enough? Do I not show that I love him by the things I do for him?* These were all questions she had asked a thousand times but could never quite find an answer. Without saying a word to him, she left his wallet on the counter with the ring lying next to it and went to work.

Six

Clare

She kept herself busy at work by filing and checking in patients. She didn't want to think about the ring she found in his wallet. She checked her phone every chance she got, but no calls came from Jim. She wondered if he was up yet and had seen the ring sitting on the counter. If he had, he would have called, right?

Before she knew it, it was 2:00 p.m. and they were closing for the day. On the long drive home, she wondered what she'd say to him and then became more bitter and angry as she drove. He never called. Not even to say he was sorry and that he'd been stupid again, or that he loved her. By the time she pulled in and parked, her anger had escalated.

Opening the front door, she saw Kayla was already waiting for her. As she hugged her daughter, she scanned the room for Jim, but didn't see him anywhere.

"Where's Daddy, sweetheart?"

"He's sleeping in the bed. I played in my room like he told me to do."

"You are such a good girl, sweetie. Mommy loves you so much. Don't ever forget that."

"Okay. I love you too, Mommy." Clare kissed her on the cheek and marched towards the bedroom, glancing at the counter.

His ring was gone.

She entered the bedroom and stared at him; if her eyes could burn through his soul, they would have. She nudged his arm, forcing him up. She couldn't hold in her rage any longer.

"I can't believe you went to bed when you were supposed to be watching Kayla! You're an asshole, Jim!" He bolted up in bed, looking puzzled.

"Clare, I can explain."

"Explain what! That the vows we took don't mean anything to you. That it's okay for you to sleep around. I don't know what marriage means to you, but to me it means to love, honor, cherish and be faithful to one another!" Her voice rose as each word came out, then before she knew it, she was screaming at the top of her lungs. She'd held her feelings in way too long, and he deserved every bit of it.

Storming out of the bedroom, she took a couple of the wedding pictures from the living room wall and strode back into the bedroom. She set the frames down on the bed, pulled the photos out, and shoved them in his face. "This doesn't mean anything to you, does it?" she screamed again and started ripping photos into pieces. When she was finished, a pile of torn pictures lay in his lap.

"Are you done? I want you to know that I didn't sleep with anyone. I swear."

"It doesn't matter, Jim. It's the fact that you took off your ring. You were planning to sleep with someone. That's what hurts the most." Tears streamed down her cheeks. She couldn't live this life anymore; she just wanted to run and hide from the pain that he caused.

She turned and stormed into the bathroom, closing the door behind her. Five minutes later, she came out, went into the closet, and changed her clothes. Before she took Kayla, she told him she had to get out of the house and away from him for a while.

****

Weeks flew by, and neither one spoke a word about what happened that day. Clare just wanted to put it behind her, though it was easier said than done. She poured herself into her work and tried to pretend he didn't exist.

On March 21st, they went to court for his DUI. Jim was put on a six-month probation without a driver's license as long as the fines were paid in full. Once more, he was spared from going to jail. He'd go to work, hang out at Juan Garcia's house afterwards, and come home late. Clare and Jim didn't see much of each other; it was as if they never left Ohio.

Clare went to work as often as she could and took Kayla to the beach on the weekends.

****

On one Saturday evening, Clare gave Kayla a bath and put her to bed. Jim wasn't home yet, so she decided to take a hot shower and crawled into bed, then shut off her cell phone before lying down.

Hours later, Clare heard the bedroom door squeak open and pretended to be asleep. She shot a glance at the clock next to the bed to see what time it was. Jim fumbled around and made his way over to Clare.

"Clare, are you up?" His words slurring as he nudged her. "I can't do this anymore, Clare." Something hard hit her leg. Pain in her shin jolted her to sit up. That's when she saw the gun in his hand.

"What are you doing, Jim?" She blurted out as she jumped out of bed. "Where did you get that?"

"I can't live like this anymore, Clare. I'm going to kill myself. You and Kayla are better off without me." He stumbled backwards and went into the kitchen. Grabbing the phone, he made his way to the balcony and dialed a number. Clare checked on Kayla and then went outside and sat next to Jim, thinking of a way to get the gun from his hand. Jim handed the phone to her.

"Who is it?" she asked putting the receiver to her ear. "Hello? Who is this?"

"Are you his wife?" the man asked.

"Yes. Who is this?"

"I'm the dispatcher. Your husband called 911. Is everything okay? What's going on there?"

"I don't know. He came home drunk and started ranting about us not deserving him—he has a gun!"

"Is there anyone else in the house?"

70

"Yes, my daughter. She's sleeping in another room."

"You need to get out of the house now. There are police officers surrounding your house and more on the way. Go to the door and walk outside."

Clare wept as she hurried to the front door. Jim paced back and forth in the living room with the gun swinging in the air. After opening the door, Clare saw five squad cars surrounding the apartment. She continued to talk on the phone and then an officer in the distance informed her that she was talking to one of them and to hang up the phone.

"Get behind us!" one of the officers shouted.

She screamed. "My daughter is in there! What about my daughter?" Fear flowed through her body as she hurried down the sidewalk.

"We'll get her out. Stand behind us so we can reach your husband."

Clare ran out through the door and crouched behind the officer, but she couldn't see the door to the front of the condo because tall bushes blocked her view. She watched as two officers made their way to the back of the condominium. There had to be at least ten officers surrounding the place, but all she could think about was

Kayla. She couldn't care less what happened to Jim; she just didn't want him to touch Kayla.

An officer to the far right of her had a straight shot at the front door. He called out to Jim asking him to set the gun down and come outside. Jim staggered out and dropped to the ground on his knees, then he placed his arms over his head and lay down. Four officers raced over, held him down, and cuffed him. They pulled him up and pushed him to one of the squad cars, then tossed him in the back seat.

Clare couldn't look at him. Her stomach tied in knots as she raced inside the house. Opening Kayla's door, she tiptoed in to make sure she wasn't hurt. She was surprised that she hadn't woken up with all the chaos going on outside her door.

Several officers searched the condo and asked Clare questions. She signed endless forms stating what went on that night and one giving permission for the police to hold all of Jim's hunting guns. She didn't want any guns left in the house after tonight.

"Officer Dean?" she asked. "I don't know where that gun came from. We don't own a gun like that."

Officer Dean held the gun up. "This is a .357 Magnum. You say you don't own this gun?"

"Yes, that's not Jim's." Taking a seat, she said, "He came home with that tonight. The only place he has been hanging out is at his friend's house, Juan Garcia, a guy from work." The officer wrote everything down in his two-by-three notepad.

"I'll check out the serial number and we'll find the owner," he told her. "Are you going to be all right?"

"Yeah, I'll be fine now. Where are you taking him? Is he going to jail?"

"No, he's not going to jail, not this time. He will be going to a suicide ward for drug and alcohol abuse. He will get the help he needs, but it will be up to him on the drinking. He should go to AA and attend meetings." The officer handed her a pamphlet about the clinic where Jim would be staying. She glanced through it and set it on the counter.

"I've seen that place on Golden Gatte, I just didn't know what it was, until now."

"Daniel Penning is a great place to go when you are having these kinds of problems."

"Oh, one of those places."

"Just to let you know, down here we don't take drinking or domestic violence lightly. Here's my card if you need anything. We'll keep his guns in safekeeping, so hold onto this paper if you want to get them out. Only you will be able to retrieve them. This way he can't walk in and try to take them."

Clare thanked Officer Dean once more and saw him out. As she locked the door behind him, she stopped in the kitchen to for a glass of water. It was already past 4:00 a.m. and was glad that she didn't have to work that weekend. Maybe she could get some sleep before Kayla woke up.

****

Day light came too soon as Clare stared at the clock next to the bed. Kayla hadn't come into the room yet, so she closed her eyes to catch a little more sleep. An hour later, she was up and making coffee.

She decided that they would go visit Grammy for a while and then maybe go to the park. Clare wished she had some friends to hang out with while Jim was away, but it was something she hadn't got around to since they'd arrived.

She called her mom in Ohio, telling her everything was fine, and they were going to the park later. There was no way she could tell them what was going on down here, at least not yet. It was too much for Clare to handle, and telling her parents would only make things worse. Besides, she'd been keeping these secrets from them all along. They never even wanted her to leave, but they knew that it was Jim's wish to move down here. Now, Clare was all alone in a state where she had no family or friends, and phoning them wasn't the same.

She bent over and scooped up Kayla into her arms, planting kisses all over her face and hugging her tight; not wanting to let her go. Kayla never asked where Daddy was, and Clare wasn't about to tell her.

****

Clare had made several trips to visit Jim in the past few weeks, and tomorrow they were letting him come home. She didn't tell him about the guns being removed from the house, but she did ask where he'd found the .357 Magnum.

Jim hesitated, at first but explained that he had taken the gun from Juan Garcia's house before leaving for the bar that night. She said the police were going to find out

75

who the gun belonged to and that he'd better hope Juan Garcia didn't press charges for stealing his gun.

Jim arrived home from rehab and told Clare that he had called Cable and Sons who had kept his job open for him, but told them he didn't want it anymore, and would find another job. Clare wished he had found other work before quitting, but she knew his mind was already made up and when that happened there was no use trying to change it. Jim always did whatever he wanted anyway, with or without her consent. On the odd occasion, he did ask her, he always did the total opposite. She never understood why he bothered asking her for her opinion if he wasn't going to take it.

After dinner that night, there was a knock on the door. Clare got up to answer it, hoping it wasn't the police. Her face froze when she opened the door.

"Hello, Clare. Thought I'd surprise you."

"Brenda Boyles, what are you doing here?" Clare had met Brenda at the factory back in Ohio, two years ago. Clare had been going through things with Jim's drinking, so she kept to herself, but Brenda was the one who started talking to her. They had become good friends as the months passed by, but Clare held things in and wasn't sure how much she should confide in Brenda. She had few friends, but that was because of her trust issue.

"I've missed you, and I've always wanted to live in Florida, so I packed up everything and here I am."

Clare invited her along, with her daughter Samantha, into the living room. Jim took a second look and frowned.

"Well, hello Brenda." Jim painted on a smile. "What brings you down here?"

"I was telling Clare that I had always wanted to live here, so what better time to do it than now. Besides, I missed my best friend."

"What about your job and a place to live?"

"I quit my job and sold what I didn't need or want anymore, I'm hoping to find a place down here I can afford. I shouldn't have any problem getting a job."

"So, you don't have a place to live?" Jim asked.

"Well, no. I was hoping that we could sleep on your sofa for a while? You know, until I get a job and look for a place to live."

Clare and Jim glanced at each other. Clare knew he wouldn't like the thought of her living with them, what with everything that had been going on. She was nervous and scared, but relieved to have a friend to lean on.

Clare turned back to Brenda. "I guess that's fine with us, but this place is pretty small. Maybe we could get a bigger place and share the rent until you save up for your own home."

Brenda flipped her straight brown hair over her shoulder. "That sounds good to me. We can also split the utilities, since we'll be living together."

Jim reached for his cell phone and walked onto the porch. Moments later he came back in beaming.

"Ken Watts has another condo we can look at. It has three bedrooms and he'll charge the same for rent if you'd like to look at it tomorrow." Jim sat back down on the rose brocade sofa and continued his conversation with Ken.

"Great! I have tomorrow off. See what time he can meet us there."

Jim conveyed the message to Ken and closed his phone. "11:00 a.m. okay with you?"

Clare cleared her throat. "Sounds good to me. Do you want to go with us?" she asked Brenda.

"Sure, I just got here, so I have nothing scheduled yet. After we're done, I'll go fill out applications around Naples."

****

That evening, Samantha slept in Kayla's room and Brenda made her bed on the sofa. After chatting with Clare, they unloaded what Brenda would need for the night. Clare told her about recent events. She needed someone to confide in and Brenda showing up when she did was a prayer answered. They had a lot to catch up on. Brenda knew some of the problems Jim had caused in Ohio, but Clare didn't tell her everything.

Before they knew it, it was 1:00 a.m. and they decided to call it a night. Jim had gone to bed hours ago while they talked. He didn't care for Brenda much, but recognized the need for Clare to have a friend here.

****

The next morning, they met Ken Watts at the apartment near Tamiami Trail on Breech Road and walked around the duplex he had for rent. They would be sharing a driveway with another couple who lived on the other side. Walking in the front door, they entered the living room and saw that it was wide open to the dining room and kitchen with white walls and cabinets. In every place down here seemed to have white cabinet and walls. *Must be a Florida thing*, Clare thought.

An attachment off the duplex was made into a laundry room, but it was big enough for Clare to put the girl's beds in. It had a slider dividing the room from the living room. Down the hall were two bedrooms; the bigger one would be Jim and Clare's since they were on the lease. Brenda took the back bedroom, which wasn't very large, but since she'd only be sleeping in it, it didn't matter. The rooms were more spacious than the condo they were living in now.

Taking a second look around, Clare, Jim, and Brenda were satisfied with the place and signed the contract with Ken. He offered to let them move in that weekend if they wanted.

Now all Clare had to do was start packing. Even though most of their things were in a storage unit, with this bigger space, she'd be able to get everything out of storage and save them money every month.

Seven

Present time...

I remember meeting my best friend for the first time. We worked together at a factory making kitchen cabinets. She didn't know I saw her sitting in her car one night and that I knew what her husband was doing to her. No one dared to ask how she was doing, but I, on the other hand, wanted to be her friend and make it all go away.

I was sitting in the cafeteria talking to some of my friends when I saw her come through the door. Her eyes were red and puffy from crying. She held her head down so no one would notice, but I did. I noticed everything about her and that night I would get her to talk to me. I don't know if that makes me nosy, but to be honest, I don't care what people think of me; I never have. Most of the people at the factory just turned their heads the other way and didn't ask.

She had just started work there a few weeks after I did. Our boss gave her a shitty ass job, but only because his girlfriend was jealous of her. Sure, she was beautiful, but she didn't bother anyone, and so what if he was attracted to her. That didn't give his girlfriend the right to have him stick Clare in a room by herself, but it didn't last more than a couple of months because she ended up with tendinitis in both her arms from taping boxes all night.

Clare was then moved to an inspector's job. I worked right behind her, making drawers for the cabinets coming down the line. I watched every move she made that night before lunch break. I introduced myself. We talked all through lunch and every day after that.

One night her name was echoing through the loud speaker to report upstairs. Her face flushed red as she glanced around to see if anyone was staring at her. After being relieved from her post, she headed up to see what they wanted, but she only returned for a second to get her bag and then left. The next night she told me what had happened. Why she had to leave.

When she got home the house was dark, she fumbled for the light and switched it on. She said she crept into the living room and found her husband lying on the sofa with a 9mm gun lying on the floor next to him. She ran over to him to see if he had killed himself, but all he did was moan and tell her to leave him alone. She didn't see any blood, so she picked up the gun and hid it in their bedroom.

Out in the kitchen there was a bottle of pills scattered on the counter, which she cleaned up. She spent the night crying herself to sleep and praying to God that he would just stop drinking.

He seemed to be drinking every few days, but I only saw her come to work once with a bruise on her face. Although she claimed she ran into a door, I knew better, so I told her that she could be honest with me because I wouldn't tell a soul. She told me that she got it from protecting her daughter. She said she was trying to leave and take them both to her parent's house. He had forced himself into the back seat before she had a chance to lock the doors, but then he grabbed their daughter. She flung herself into the back of the car and that was when he punched her in the face. She tried to cover the bruise, but I could see it through the makeup she'd applied.

A week later, she was called back upstairs because he had been in an accident. This time he had ran his truck into a tree by their garage. She was talking to a police officer on the phone and he requested she come home at once.

When she arrived, the police were at her house trying to get him to calm down, but he just kept walking around as three officers followed him like a lost puppy. They ended up taking him, into rehab at some hospital and left her at home to clean up his mess.

She wanted to leave him, but though he wasn't working that much she couldn't make it without his paycheck. She scanned newspapers finding places she could afford, but then he would promise her that he would stop drinking, so she stayed. Sometimes it lasted weeks, even months, but he always went back to drinking.

There were three plants the company owned. Jim worked at Plant One, which was right down the road from Plant two where we worked. Clare started earlier than he did, so she wasn't able to verify if he was going to work when he said he was. We always knew when he didn't go because he would call the plant asking her to come home. He'd say that he needed her, and it was always an emergency. *But* every time she went home, he'd either be passed out or there were cops waiting for her.

I have only met Jim a couple of times, but I'll never forget his face, or what he has done to her.

Eight

Clare

Since Brenda showed up, Jim had stopped drinking. He'd decided to get help and go to AA. Jim went to meetings almost every night. He began hanging out with several people from AA, going out after meetings and talking to a sponsor every day.

Clare quit her job at the Immediate Care and landed work at a chiropractor's office, where she didn't have to go in on the weekends.

Jim had found a job at a Marina on Marco Island working Friday to Monday, and this was one of the reasons Clare found a new job. She was able to locate a daycare two streets away for Kayla, which made it easier to pick her up and drive to Marco Island for Jim on the days he worked.

Learning a new job had become frustrating for Clare. She had trouble remembering and had to be told several times, what she had forgot. She felt like her mind was slipping away, and there was nothing she could do to control it. She liked her new job at the chiropractor's office, but most days she worked until 6:00 p.m. This became a problem for the daycare as it closed at the same time and they didn't like the fact that she was always running late.

To make matters worse, living with Brenda for a couple of months hadn't worked out. She ended up leaving due to not paying her share of the rent and utilities. Jim was furious one day when Brenda came home from shopping and had bought several new DVDs. She had claimed she didn't have any money for the rent, so Jim told her she had to find another place. Clare was okay with the idea since she was busy running all over town dropping Jim off at work by 6:00 a.m., back to Naples to get ready for work and then taking Kayla to daycare.

****

A couple of weeks later, Jim was back to his usual tricks. He met some friends at the marina, and they drank; Jim must have felt left out and started drinking again.

Clare's phone rang at work. Jim said he was spending his day fishing at the pier down at the beach, but he called saying that he needed her to meet him and his mom at the impound lot on Lake Street. When Clare asked what had happened, he explained that when he went to buy an identification card for fishing, the woman behind the counter at the Department of Motor Vehicles, stated that it was not a driver's license and added, "**DO NOT DRIVE WITH IT.**" Failing to register what she'd just told him, he got in the jeep and pulled out of the parking space. Seconds later, as he passed the building, a police car pulled him over, putting him in handcuffs.

Clare was hysterical and spent her lunch getting the jeep out of the lot where the police had it towed. Of course, they didn't take checks, so she had to run to the bank and withdraw two hundreds in cash. Jim told her that in a couple of weeks they'd have to go to court. She just bottled her feelings up inside, waiting for them to explode.

****

A week later, she was going through the classifieds looking for a new job. Her boss had told her that work was more important than family, but Clare didn't care for his comment and told him that she disagreed. She had always fulfilled her hours at work, though there were a few times when she altered the schedule. She was dependable, but he had a cow when she couldn't stay past 6:00 p.m. Only on two occasions did a patient show up at 5:30 p.m., but she had taken their co-pay ahead of time, so there was no reason for her to stay. She had done all the paperwork, and the other doctor staying late said he didn't object to her leaving to pick up Kayla.

She stopped when she came across an ad in the paper for a receptionist, the fax number belonged to her boss. Her heart sank. She knew they would eventually replace her after the intense argument they'd had.

On the computer, she composed a letter to the chiropractor stating that she will be giving him her two weeks' notice. She spent Sunday looking through the paper for another job, making copies of her resume, and faxing them to the numbers included in the classifieds.

The next morning she put the letter on her boss's desk and started work while waiting for him to come in. He arrived fifteen minutes later and called her into his office.

"What's this all about?"

"You must think I'm stupid," Clare blurted out. "I saw your ad in the paper for a new receptionist."

"Oh." His head fell.

"Don't worry about it, I'm already looking for a new job, I'll work my two weeks." *I don't care anymore, so let him find someone new*, she thought. Leaving his office, she started working on the new paperwork for a new patient who was coming in that morning.

Friday came and she sat working at her desk when the doctor came over to tell her that he wouldn't need her to come in on Monday because he was letting her go.

Her heart raced. "But I still have another week left."

"We filled your position yesterday, so we don't need you anymore," he said with a grin.

She sat there for a few seconds thinking over what had just happened, she then collected her things and clocked out. It was only 3:00 p.m. but she figured what the hell; if she wasn't coming back on Monday, why stay?

She raced out of the door and drove to the store where Grammy worked. Tears filled her eyes as she made her way there. She'd never been without a job and the thought frightened her. *How could he do this when I had another week left?*

She wiped away the tears that streamed down her face. She didn't know how they would pay the bills without a paycheck, and she hadn't heard back from any of the places where she'd sent her resume.

She parked the car and bolted into the store where she saw Grammy hanging blouses on a stand near the back.

She waved to Clare as she came towards her, Clare burst into tears.

"What's wrong, sweetie?"

"I've lost my job. He let me go a week early. I don't know what to do. How will we pay the bills?" Things she never thought of came pouring out of her. She was sobbing so much that she started to hyperventilate.

"Take it easy, Clare," Grammy tried to calm her while rubbing the small of her back.

Clare took several deep breaths and wiped her nose with the Kleenex Grammy handed her. "I have never been fired before. I had things figured out with my last check, and now we'll be short."

"You'll figure it out, just have faith. Have you told Jim yet?"

"No! I came here first. I don't know how to tell him."

"Well, you'll have to tell him, Clare. You will both work through this, like you do everything else."

"But we're running out of money, Mom. The bills have been piling up because of all the fines we had to pay so he didn't have to spend time in jail. I try to pay them, but there are just too many. He wasn't working and the job he has now is only four days a week, so there's just not enough money coming in."

Grammy embraced her and whispered in her ear, "Let me talk to Papa Benny, I think he can help you."

After thanking her, she left, picked up Kayla, then drove out to Marco Island to get Jim. On the drive home, she thought about how she would tell him. The last thing she wanted was to cause him to drink again.

Clare started to cook dinner for all of them as Jim sat watching TV. She knew she had to bring it up, and wanted to get it over with. She came into the living room and she sat down beside him.

"We need to talk," she said. Starting from the beginning, she told him what the doctor had said to her and that she was already looking for another job. As she studied his face, she thought he didn't look concerned. He wasn't upset with her losing her job.

"I think you should start your own cleaning business. You could make good money if you charge twenty or more an hour."

Pondering on what he'd told her, she decided that he was right. After dinner, she created business cards on the computer and would spend Monday distributing them.

Coming up with a name for her business wasn't hard, since she actually enjoyed cleaning.

"What do you think about, 'Clean and Spotless'? The slogan will say, 'Your house will be so clean, it will be spotless'!"

"Wow! That sounds great, but that's going to be hard to live up to."

"Not really, Jim. I'm really picky. I would treat each house as though it was mine and clean it as if they were going to check everything I do." She hadn't felt this confident about anything in a long time.

****

Monday came, and she dropped off Kayla at daycare and then Jim at work. She spent the whole day driving up one end of Route 41 and down the other, by the time she was done hanging her business card in three quarters of the stores, it was time to pick up Kayla and Jim again.

It would take some time before she landed a job cleaning, but she was good at getting her hopes up and then feeling bad about it later.

****

By Wednesday, she had received three calls on the faxes she sent out for a medical billing job. After the interviews, she was hired at a Dermatology Clinic on Goodlette Drive, which was one street away from their home. She was to start that coming Monday.

She also received a call from Papa Benny asking if she was interested in a cleaning job where he managed a community full of homes. She felt a weight being lifted from her shoulders as she answered with enthusiasm. That night their property owner called offering her a job cleaning the house next door to theirs and would pay her twenty dollars an hour.

It's finally happening, she thought. *Things are going to get better for us.*

Nine

Jim

Jim sat on a stool guzzling his beer. He tried not to think about what Clare was doing; he just wanted to be alone and enjoy himself. It's all he'd known since growing up, drinking on the weekends and going to parties. His girlfriend before he met Clare, now, she understood him; at least she didn't say his drinking bothered her.

Gazing around the empty bar, he guzzled down the rest of his beer and ordered another. It was past 5:00 p.m. and Clare was off cleaning homes again. *She never seems to spend any time with me*, he thought. *Always off doing something with Kayla or working.*

The door to the bar opened and a couple of girls walked in laughing. Jim smiled at the blonde-haired woman as they took a table near the back. He swiveled around and watched them. He held up his beer to the bartender letting him know he needed another one. When the bartender came over, Jim asked what the blonde girl was having and ordered her a drink.

It didn't surprise him that she came over and sat next to him—it was his plan to begin with.

He slid off his ring and shoved it in his pants pocket. After talking for hours, she told her friends that she was going for a ride and would see them later.

Jim wasn't supposed to be driving, but didn't think much of it. He drove all the time in Ohio. Besides, he'd be careful and not get caught. The woman climbed in the jeep and they drove to her place, stopping for a case of beer on the way.

Laughing and joking, they sat on the leather sofa in her living room. She twirled her finger in a lock of hair and smiled. Jim stood up, nearly falling over, then staggered to the bathroom.

Looking in the mirror, he fixed his hair and returned to the room, but she was gone. As he was standing there staring at the photos on the wall, the blonde girl walked up behind him, wrapped her arms around his waist, and undid the button on his jeans. He turned to her and pressed his lips against hers. Breathing heavily as they undressed each other, he rubbed her breasts and kissed them as he made his way down her chest to her stomach, licking and kissing every inch of her body.

Throwing her on the sofa, he straddled her and forced himself into her. She moaned as she felt him inside her. Jim went down on her, making her release repeatedly, while stroking himself. She got on her knees to satisfy him in return.

They lay together on the sofa and eventually went to her bedroom where they embraced each other again and again.

****

The next morning he woke up and found himself in someone else's house and in someone else's bed, but whose? He heard a door shut in the next room. Throwing the blankets off, he realized he wasn't wearing anything. He glanced around the room, but didn't see his clothes. He wrapped the sheet around himself and ventured through the door.

Whoever it was had left him a note on his folded clothes.

Thanks for the awesome night, had to go into work this morning.

Call me.

Broken Promises

239–555–2343

Shannon Crumb

Jim read the note three times before putting his clothes back on and hurried out of the door. Thinking back, he couldn't remember much of anything from last night, except the blonde-haired girl from the bar and getting in his jeep. He couldn't remember if she left with him or where they went—everything was a blur.

Looking at the clock on the dashboard, he saw it was going on 6:30 a.m. He raced home, hoping Clare would still be asleep and not ask him any questions.

When he arrived home, he opened the door to the bedroom and peered in. He slid in next to her, as if she would think he'd been there all night.

Ten

Clare

She heard Jim open the front door, but she pretended to be asleep. She had got up several times during the night, pacing back and forth, wondering where he was and who he was with. Every time she called his cell phone, it went straight to voicemail. She didn't sleep as much as she had hoped, but knowing he was probably with someone else made her nauseous.

Moving slightly, she held her finger to her nose after smelling the aroma of beer from his body. He told her that he wouldn't drink anymore and wouldn't sleep around, but she knew he was never going to change. Everything ran through her mind at that moment. Things she'd forgotten about and things she didn't want to remember. *But* nothing was going to slip from her memory that easily; she'd never forget the things he'd done, and she wouldn't let him live them down. She loved him didn't he know that? Didn't he care about her the way she cared about him? Trying not to move, she lay there waiting for him to fall asleep before getting up and going into the kitchen.

Kayla had spent the night with her Grammy, so Clare could work late cleaning. The house needed to be done in two days, so she stayed until she finished it last night. She thought Jim had to work, but apparently, he had other plans in mind, and those plans included him drinking and sleeping with someone else. She didn't know for sure that he was with another woman, but what else could he have been doing when he didn't come home last night?

Drinking coffee was her only distraction until she finally walked into the bedroom and took his clothes from the floor to wash the stink out of them. As she lifted his jeans, she heard something hit the floor. She got on her knees and swept the carpet until she was holding his ring in her fingers. Her heart felt as if it had been wrenched out of her chest. She slipped the band on her finger and left the room.

She stared at the ring while throwing his clothes in the washer. All the same questions came racing back at her. Tears slid down her face as she decided to get dressed and go to Grammy's house.

They sat outside on the lanai and she poured out her heart. Clare told Grammy about Jim not coming home and that he was sleeping around again. Grammy held Clare in her arms, saying she was sorry for her son acting like this and treating her the way he was.

Clare wiped her face and picked up Kayla's belongings as she headed to the door, then hugged Grammy one more time.

"Thank you for listening," Clare said.

"You're welcome, sweetie. I know my son has his faults, but he's still my son. I wish you wouldn't come here and tell me about the things he's done. It makes me sick to my stomach knowing what he is doing to you and to his family."

The words were like a bee sting to her heart. Clare rushed out of the door with Kayla. *How could she say that to me? I needed someone to talk to, and she knows I don't have many friends down here, or any family for that matter. Why would she say something like that?* Her heart ached worse now than it did when she got there.

She decided not to go home; instead, she went to the beach for a couple of hours. She needed to think things through before saying anything to him. It's one thing that he's drinking, but it's another matter when he's sleeping with other women.

Her heart was breaking more now than it had before. The trust she felt for him was gone, but the love was still there. She didn't know why or how she could still want a person like that. Spending time with her daughter was all she could do to keep herself sane. She didn't want to go home anytime soon; she didn't want to face him and hurt any more than she was. She didn't want him to touch her or be near her. She needed time away; she wanted to go home to her parents.

Clare called Brenda to ask if she could come over for a while with Kayla and that she needed to use her computer.

Arriving twenty minutes later, she explained what had happened since that morning. Clare browsed for tickets online to go visit her family in Ohio for a week. After searching the Internet, she sat outside with Brenda while Kayla and Samantha played in the living room.

"What are you going to say to him?" Brenda asked.

"I'm not sure. I have to give him his ring back, but I don't want to know where he was last night. Don't get me wrong, I do care, but it just makes me sick inside realizing he was with someone else."

"You have to say something to him, Clare. You can't just let him get away with this."

"You're right, but still…"

"Still what? What are you so afraid of, Clare?"

"I'm not afraid!"

"Yes, you are. You are not telling me something. Come on, we've been friends for two years now. What's bugging you? You know you can talk to me."

"I know I can talk to you."

"So, what's on your mind? You can tell me anything, Clare."

"I just want him to stop. Stop drinking and stop being with other women. Just stop doing what he's been doing. I love him and knew when I married him that he was the one I wanted to spend the rest of my life with, but now…now I'm not sure. I never thought he'd pick up a drink when I met him. I never knew what he was like before; if I had, then I wouldn't have married him in the first place. He was so sweet, kind, and loving, but now he's like Satan's child. He's turned into a mean and selfish person since he started drinking."

"Don't forget the suicide attempts."

"How could I forget them? There have been so many I've lost count. You know, if he did ever kill himself, how could I live with that. How can I tell Kayla her dad's never coming back? I would blame myself if he did. For one, he always says it's my fault that he drinks and that our marriage is falling apart."

"You know better than that, Clare. I hope you don't believe all those lies he's telling you. You go out and bust your ass working to pay all the bills. You take care of Kayla, the house, the groceries—and him. He should be the one out there supporting the family, not you. All he cares about is himself, and you know that. Jim this and Jim that. Jim wants this and Jim wants that, but if he doesn't get it, he goes out and gets hammered. He then he comes home takes it out on you, and says that you're the worthless one. Don't get suckered into his world anymore, Clare, you're better than that."

"I know, but I have Kayla to take care of and rent down here isn't cheap. How can I afford to raise her and give her what she needs?"

"Start putting money aside."

"Oh, trust me. Every time I start to, he stops working and I have to use the money to pay bills. I have tried to save money, but with him it's a no-win situation."

"Were you able to purchase tickets to fly home?"

"No." Clare took a sip of her coffee. "They cost more than I was willing to spend right now. I'll go, but not right now; I just can't afford it."

"Oh, by the way, I found another condo for rent. I've been working with this realtor and he said I could rent from him and wouldn't have to pay much. The condo has two bedrooms and a den.

If you're willing to leave Jim, we could split the rent and you could save money for your own place."

"That sounds tempting, but I don't know if he'd even let me leave."

"What do you mean?" Brenda took a sip and set down her coffee cup.

"Well, he has threatened me before when I tried in Ohio, so I've been afraid ever since. He said I'd never see Kayla again if I tried to leave."

"And you believe him?"

"I have no reason not to."

"I think he is using Kayla to get to you. Besides, why would he sleep with other women if he wanted you around? I don't wish to sound mean, but you've got to be blind not to see it, Clare."

"He wouldn't do that." Clare looked away, thinking of all of Jim's acts of betrayal. She was certain he loved Kayla and would never hurt her. *Why would he use her to get to me?* Shaking the thought from her head, she finished her coffee and told Brenda it was time for them to leave.

"Clare, I'm sorry if I said something offensive. I care about you and don't want you wounded anymore."

"I know, but I just can't leave right now. I have to try to make it work. Something has gone wrong in every relationship I've had. It's taken me this long to marry and have a child that I was told I'd never be able to have. It's what I've always wanted. I just can't walk away from this yet; besides, Kayla still needs her dad."

"Yes, she does, but not one that drinks and sleeps around. What kind of marriage is that? I'm just saying, think about this, Clare, and when you're ready I'll be here to pick you up."

"Thanks, Brenda, but I need to fix this myself. I need to get him to understand and quit drinking."

Brenda let out a bitter laugh. "You can't fix it, Clare. Only he can do that."

Clare stood and gathered up Kayla, then said goodbye as she headed out of the condo.

"Clare, wait! All I want you to do is think this over and all that he is doing. Stop letting him control you and be happy."

"I am happy!" she insisted, holding back the tears. "I just want him to stop."

Brenda put her arms around her and held her tightly. "I know you do, I'm sorry." Brenda held Clare until she stopped crying.

"Thanks, I needed that. I've been fighting these tears for so long. I feel like I'm going to burst, but I won't let him see me like this."

"Maybe he should. Maybe he needs to see you cry because it shows you care."

"Maybe, but I feel better now. We should go. Thanks for listening, Brenda."

"Anytime, Clare. That's what friends are for."

Clare went out of the door and buckled Kayla into the back seat. On the drive home, she replayed their conversation in her head and rehearsed what she'd say to Jim. She needed to sit down and talk to him, to make him understand what was at stake, and find out how he felt about their relationship.

When she got home, Jim's phone was beeping. She opened it and noticed there were several messages from a number she didn't recognize. Pushing the voicemail key, she was asked for a pin number. Her pulse pumped through her body. He had put on a security number to keep her from listening to his messages. *He's never done that before,* she thought.

Setting down the phone, she hurried into the bedroom. Jim wasn't in bed. She turned to the sound of water shutting off. After tapping on the bathroom door, she entered and announced that they were home. Jim stood there with a towel around him.

"Hey, where've you been all day?"

"Oh, we went to your mother's and then visited Brenda. Did you just get up?"

"A little while ago. Thought I'd freshen up a bit."

"Jim, can we talk?"

"Sure, what's on your mind?" Bending over he put on his boxers and then his tan khaki shorts. She had forgotten how good-looking he was naked, a little thin, but he still had a nice body. Her eyes fixated on his neck.

A hickey!

Shaking the image from her head, she hesitated, then pulled the ring off her finger and handed it over to him. "I found this in the jeans you wore last night."

Looking like he was caught with his hand in the cookie jar, he sat down on the toilet.

"Clare, I can explain. I went out yesterday when you were working and well… well, I had an excessive amount to drink. I know I was sober and going to AA, but I needed a drink. There's no excuse for my drinking, I'm sorry."

"And the ring? What was it doing in your jeans and not on your finger?"

"I don't remember that part. I don't honestly know how it got there. I don't remember much from last night."

"Where did you sleep, because you certainly didn't sleep here last night?" Putting one hand on her hip, she rubbed her forehead with the other and tried to release the headache coming on.

"There was this woman at the bar, and I think she persuaded me to go to her house. I think…."

"You think what?"

"I think she raped me, Clare." His face looked like a sad puppy dog begging for food.

Clare burst out laughing, but inside her heart broke. "Women don't rape men. They seduce them, but they don't rape them, you asshole!"

"She did, Clare, I swear I'm telling you the truth."

"Then why do you have a hickey on your neck? You may believe your story, but I don't. I don't believe anything you tell me anymore. And by the way, she's been calling you all day." She was assuming it was the woman calling, but since she wasn't able to listen to the messages, she was accusing him before knowing if it were true. What he said to her was bull crap, and she was getting tired of his games.

Clare stepped outside and watched Kayla play in the sand near the steps. Neither one spoke a word after that day about what he told her, nor did she ask him about the messages. She figured he would have denied it if there was someone else.

****

Two months later, Jim suggested they find another place to rent. He said he had heard about some break-ins on the next street and thought it was best they find a new place to live. They spoke to the property owner who told them they could end their lease as long as they found someone else to rent it.

After agreeing, Clare put an ad in the local newspaper and within a week, they had someone interested. Clare showed the duplex to a couple younger than they were with a baby; she took them through the rooms and then walked them out to their car. Within twenty minutes, the property owner called and told them that they would take over their lease. After hanging up the phone, she called Jim on his cell and let him know the good news.

That night they looked at three different apartments for rent. The last one astounded Clare. It was smaller than the duplex, but was brand new and in a better neighborhood. They were asking for a hundred dollars more a month than their current place.

The man told them that it was just finished and that they were the first to see it.

Jim and Clare discussed the rent and decided they would take it. It was in a much nicer area than the last two places they'd lived in.

After signing the papers, they were told that in two weeks they could move in, which was good for Clare because she still needed to pack. Thinking back, she couldn't believe they had only been in Florida for seven months and they'd be moving for the third time.

Eleven

Clare

A month had passed by since their move. Clare finished unpacking within days and was building up her new business. She designed flyers and heard about a newspaper offering ads that didn't cost very much, so she paid for eight weeks' worth.

She was let go from the dermatologist clinic because of some mistakes that had surfaced. It happened so quickly, but they wouldn't listen when she said it wasn't her fault. The first incident happened when several patients came in at the same time for their appointments. Two girls who worked there tried to help, but they didn't pull out all the files for Clare to check off and give to the nurse. One lady ended up sitting in the waiting room for an hour and a half. Clare noticed her and asked if she was waiting for someone, but when Clare heard her name, she realized the woman had been overlooked. She pulled out her file and gave it to the nurse, but was then questioned why it was put there so late. Clare explained exactly what had happened.

The nurse said they could squeeze the woman in, but whispered angrily to Clare that it wasn't to happen again.

The second incident occurred when Clare was put in charge after two weeks. She forgot to put the money envelope in the drawer after finishing some paperwork. She left to clean a condo and then remembered, so she called the clinic and told the owner who answered the phone. Terrified, she explained the situation to the doctor, but was relieved when she said it would be taken care of.

She returned to work the following Monday, and everything appeared to be fine, until Clare was called into the office after 3:00 p.m. They let her go with two weeks' severance pay. Clare tried to explain, but they had made their decision; there was nothing she could say to change their mind.

Driving home, she called Jim to let him know what had happened only to find out he'd lost his job at the marina. When he went to court for driving under suspension, the judge gave him two ultimatums: he could either work seven weekends doing community service, which equaled to fourteen days, or pay off all the fines and serve fourteen straight days in jail. He ended up only serving twelve days in jail, but that was after he spent one weekend performing community service, which was cleaning up garbage on the highways. He came home complaining about how hot it was and that there was no way in hell he was going to spend any more weekends cleaning up people's trash. He called the attorney, but was told he'd have to go to jail if he didn't want to do it. So he did.

Clare had to ask Papa Benny for the court's money, but she worked as much as she could to pay him back the two grand. She'd already forked out over four grand for the DUI he received in February and now had to pay out even more for Jim's ignorance.

When was it all going to stop? Money was going out left and right. The only good thing to come out of it was Jim joining AA again. Now was this his fourth or fifth attempt, she couldn't recall. He still blamed her each time he fell off the wagon and told her they needed to figure out how to make more money. She'd scream at him that if he wasn't fired or quit his job, then maybe they'd have more money. Without more cleaning jobs there was nothing she could do.

****

A hurricane was on the verge of sweeping through Naples, so Clare gathered up a few articles of clothing and other essentials, and they all headed to Grammy's place where they had hurricane shutters to protect them.

The weatherman estimated that the wind gusts would be around one hundred and twenty or more miles per hour, so there would be tornados and power outages.

Kayla slept with Clare and Jim that night when the hurricane hit Naples. At 6:00 a.m., Clare woke up, but Jim wasn't next to her. Walking around the dark condo looking for him, she remembered him saying that he was going to videotape the storm. The winds were gusting, and he was outside in it—videotaping.

Kayla remained sleeping as Clare went outside to look for Jim. Her hair whipped in the wind. Palm trees bent from side to side as limbs broke off and flew through the air. Garbage cans were tipped over in the streets with trash blowing everywhere. She was only able to make it to the wall of the garage when she spotted him. He saw her and they headed back inside. Going over what he'd filmed she glanced at the video, but all she could really hear was how loud the wind sounded. The power flicked off and they were in total darkness. An hour later, the wind and rain died down, so they took a walk outside to inspect the damage.

That afternoon, Grammy, Jim, Kayla and Clare decided to take a ride out and look at the area around Naples. There was no sense in staying at the condo with no air or water.

At the beach, Clare saw nothing, but tree limbs and bamboos scattered everywhere. Houses were crushed from trees falling on them and pool screens were torn or missing. The high rises nearby were missing windows and shutters; also, parts of the building siding were gone. The stoplights they came across were all blinking red but not many people were out driving. Most had evacuated the area before the hurricane hit early that morning. Clare suggested they make a trip out to their home.

Arriving fifteen minutes later, they found the power was out at every condominium, but not too much damage was done unlike at the beach. The man who lived on the first floor had a generator hooked up outside to supply power to his place.

Clare had gone food shopping a few days before, not knowing a hurricane was coming their way, so she asked Jim to check with the man downstairs if they could plug in their refrigerator to his generator. He agreed, but only if they helped pay for the gas to run it. Clare nodded at Jim and he handed the guy a few twenties.

Taking a couple gallons of water from the refrigerator, Clare set them on the back seat of their jeep and listened to the radio broadcast about when the power would be fixed.

Two days later, the power to their place was restored and a week later, she got a job as a maintenance helper at Cayra Bay where Papa Benny managed. She was able to work the hours she needed between cleanings and pick up Kayla from daycare. By the end of December, she had accumulated thirteen clients and by January, she had over twenty.

Due to working seven days a week and ten to twelve-hour shifts, she didn't have time to do much on the weekends, so Jim took Kayla to the pool while Clare worked. The money was coming in steadily now, so she decided to put some away for an emergency. It'd drive Jim crazy if he knew they had all that money; he'd easily figure a way to spend it.

She stopped on the way home, picked up their refund check from the IRS, and deposited it into their checking account. She was hoping to get more back, to pay off some of their bills but was happy with what they had received. When they filed bankruptcy in Ohio, Jim had the idea to withdraw cash advances from the credit cards; what they didn't know was it would have to be paid back but would be written off if they purchased something. She only had a thousand left to pay on it, so she made a call to the attorney who was handling the account and paid off the rest.

Putting some clothes away, Clare heard her phone ringing and answered it.

"Hello."

"Hey, it's me Jim. Did you pick up our refund check yet?"

"Yes, I did. Why what's up?" Her heart pounded in her chest. She knew it was too good to be true.

"I'm at the Harley Davidson store with my old boss and I've always wanted a Harley. I figured since we don't have that credit card bill anymore, we could use what we were paying on it for the monthly payments of a motorcycle." A hot searing pain raced through her as she registered what he'd just suggested.

"I was hoping we could put the extra money aside, you know, for an emergency," she snapped while pacing back and forth in the living room.

"But I've always wanted one, Clare. I got a job to help pay for it and I've already checked on how much the payments would be, so I know we can afford it." He went on explaining how much he wanted the bike. Clare hoped she could talk him out of it, but she relented when he brought up spending more time together riding. She hated jumping to a decision, but his excitement made her feel hopeful and before she could say no, "yes" came rushing out.

"You won't be sorry, Clare. I'll tell the sales clerk it's a done deal. Thank you so much." She hung up the phone before she changed her mind. "Damn it! Why do I let him do that to me? Why do I have such a hard time telling him no?" she murmured.

She plopped down on the chair outside and replayed the conversation. With self-recriminations and determination to tell him no, she went back inside and reached for her phone, but it rang before she could redial Jim's number.

Startled, she answered it. "Hello."

"Hey Clare, it's me, Brenda."

"Hi, what's up?"

"I'm on my way to your place. Are you home?"

"Yeah, I'm here. Where have you been?"

She hesitated, then answered, "In Ohio."

"What were you doing there?" Sitting down on the sofa, she waited for her to respond.

"I went there because of the hurricane."

"When they said to evacuate, it didn't mean fourteen hundred miles away." She let out a laugh.

"It freaked me out, so I just drove. Look, I don't have a place t stay now and I was wondering if I could stay with you for a while? I could sleep on the sofa, just until I get a place of my own."

"What do you mean you don't have a place to live? What happened? You had a job and a condo."

"They told me not to come back if I left and I lost the condo because I didn't have enough money to pay the rent."

Clare listened with an open mind and tried not to judge her. "Sure, I guess you can stay, but we're going to talk when you get here."

"No problem, I should be there in about half an hour."

"Okay, see you then." After hanging up the phone, she organized the kitchen, gathered sheets and a blanket for Brenda, and then searched the closet for a pillow. As she set them on the end of the couch, she heard a knock at the door.

Brenda stood there with tears rolling down her face.

"What's wrong?" she asked, taking her friend by the arm and pulling her in for a hug.

Sniffling, Brenda said, "I lost her."

"Lost who, honey?" Clare pulled the box of Kleenex from the counter.

"Samantha. While I was up in Ohio, my ex-husband got custody of her. The judge said I was an unfit mother." Confused, Clare tried to put the pieces together.

"Start from the beginning, Brenda. Tell me exactly what happened." Clare listened as Brenda poured out her heart. The room fell silent when she'd finished. Clare didn't know what she could do to help. "I'm so sorry," was all she could say.

Wiping her face, Brenda nodded. "It's crazy, isn't it?"

"So, you received a letter from the court saying your ex-husband considered you a bad mother because you moved down here with her. Didn't your ex give you permission?"

"I did everything I was supposed to do with the courts, but the judge didn't like the fact that I was moving constantly, and I wasn't at a job for very long. I miss her, Clare."

"I know, sweetie, I'm so sorry. I would be lost without Kayla. Losing her would tear me apart." She thought back to when she'd had a fight with Jim a couple of weeks ago; he'd threatened again to take Kayla away from her if she ever left him. She didn't know if he was serious or just trying to scare her, but leaving wasn't something, Clare was willing to do just yet.

Jim came home an hour later, and Clare spoke to him about Brenda's circumstances. He said it would be okay for a while and that he didn't mind, but she could tell he didn't like the thought of her in their home again.

****

Weeks flew by before Brenda found a place of her own. It wasn't spectacular, but it was all she could afford. Brenda invited Clare to check out her place.

She pulled into the driveway and followed it around the back of a tan house with white trim around the

122

windows. The yard looked as if it hadn't been mowed in months and there was garbage stacked up around the sides of the house. Further around the bend, all she saw was a trailer sitting by the wood line. She came to a stop next to Brenda's van.

The trailer was one of those pop-up campers you would take camping in the summer. She was surprised it was still standing as there was so much rust on the wheel trims and the screens were covered in dirt and mold. Shaking her head in disgust, she couldn't help but feel sorry for her friend and wished she could afford something a little better than that.

Brenda opened the trailer door and shouted out to her. "Hey, I thought you would never get here."

"I had a few cleaning jobs to do, but I have time to chat until I pick up Kayla." Stepping inside, she could see a bed in the back and a door to the right, which probably led to the bathroom. The kitchen was right where she stood and had a small table. Clare took a seat inside the entrance.

"Wow, this is pretty cozy."

"You're just saying that. It's temporary. I won't be living here forever."

Thank goodness for that, Clare thought.

"I have two jobs lined up. I start one tomorrow morning and then the other in the evening."

"That's awesome, Brenda." Clare took the hair hanging down her face and stuffed it back into her ponytail.

"So, what's the morning job you have?"

"It's cleaning a bar and grill just off Davis. I have to be there by 4:00 a.m. at the latest. My job is to clean the restrooms, vacuum, and mop the floors. They're willing to pay me three hundred a week to do it."

Clare was surprised by the hours and couldn't imagine getting up that early to clean a place. She'd be too tired to finish her clients' homes and take care of Kayla, but she realized that Brenda was alone now, and she needed a better place to live in and hopefully with her daughter someday.

"I'm glad you found those jobs, also I could advertise your name to clean houses."

"That's another thing I wanted to talk to you about. You remember that realtor guy I was telling you about? He offered me several jobs cleaning condominiums before people move into them. He'll pay me twenty an hour, but thank you for the offer."

"Sure, no problem, anything to help." They sat and chatted for about an hour, then Clare hopped into her car.

"Hey, did you get a new car?"

"Yeah, I finally found a place that would take the jeep off our hands. It had over a hundred thousand miles and we still owed eight grand on it. I was able to lease this vehicle. Even though it's a little more a month, it has room for all my cleaning tools in the trunk and at least it will last longer. Jim has his license back now, so we got him a truck for five hundred off of some guy he met at AA."

"Good for you, Clare." Waving goodbye to her friend, Clare drove to the daycare center.

Entering the parking lot of their home with Kayla, her phone rang, and she spoke to a woman about cleaning her house. Before she could get out of the car, her phone rang again. To her surprise, someone else wanted their house cleaned. She couldn't believe her luck and now had over thirty clients.

Unbuckling Kayla from the car seat, she sprinted up the stairs to the third floor of their complex. She planned to make a special dinner tonight for the three of them and celebrate. She hummed along to a song as she prepared dinner and set the table.

Jim arrived a few minutes later looking glum.

Clare knew something was wrong. Her heart stopped and a knot tightened in her gut. She turned and opened the door to the refrigerator, hoping she'd read him wrong.

She made her way to Kayla's room and saw she was playing with her dolls and went back to the kitchen.

Jim was slouched on the sofa and had turned on the television.

"What's wrong, Jim? I can see something is bothering you."

"I lost my job. They said I wasn't responsible enough to work there."

Fighting back tears, she sat down and took his hand. "Tell me what happened?"

"I've just told you what they said. Why is it you don't hear me half the time!" he barked.

She released his hand and went back to the kitchen to stir the rice on the stove.

"You're worthless, Clare. I don't know why I stay with you. I can do better, you know. I don't need your shit anymore."

She kept busy by cutting up lettuce and vegetables for a salad. *I'm not worthless,* she thought, *where does he get off talking to me like that. We haven't seen or talked to each other all day, then he comes home and bam — I'm a piece of shit. I had a great day, I have several new clients, and we're going to put money aside and not have to worry.*

Jim stood up and disappeared into the bedroom. She could hear the bathroom door close and the shower turn on. She didn't feel hungry now, but finished making dinner and set everything on the table.

Preparing Kayla's plate, she shouted that it was time to eat. Jim came in and ate his meal, but the silence put Clare on edge; not knowing what he'd do or say to her next. She picked at the food on her plate, then cleaned up the dishes and got Kayla ready for a bath.

She stood in front of the mirror in Kayla's bathroom wanting to burst into tears, but instead she just stared at the woman on the other side. Touching her hair and then her face, she noticed how much weight she'd lost since they'd arrived. If she wore a slim shirt, you'd be able to see her ribs and maybe even count them. The only part she liked was how tanned she'd become, especially since it covered up the dark circles under her eyes.

She turned off the water and heard the front door close. She hurried to the slider and peered out but didn't see Jim. Wanting to relax, she opened the slider and stepped out for some air. She looked over the railing, still no Jim. His truck was sitting in the parking lot, so where did he go? She rubbed her neck as she went back inside.

By the time she'd finished giving Kayla a bath and had tucked her into bed, Jim still wasn't home. Clare watched a show on the television and then took a long hot shower before heading to bed.

She tried not to think about Jim as she forced herself to fall asleep, but she kept opening her eyes and glancing at the clock next to her. She didn't know what time she fell asleep.

That night she dreamed of the conversation they had and what he'd said to her. In her dream, she could feel something or someone watching her.

Feeling cold, she reached for the blanket to cover her up. She wasn't sure if she was still dreaming or if she was awake, but someone was standing next to her. She could see a hand reaching out to touch her. She jerked up to a sitting position and saw Jim leaning over and begin to caress her. He was removing her clothes and was touching her everywhere. Glancing at the clock next, she saw it was a couple minutes past 2:00 a.m. She wanted to stop him, but the feel of his touch excited her. She missed his touch and the way they made love. She could taste the beer as they kissed, the aroma made her turn away from him, but she still allowed him to please her.

Pain. There was so much pain as he thrust himself inside her. Squeezing her eyes shut, she tried to get her hands between her legs, but he grabbed them both and pinned her down. Tears formed in the curve of her eyes.

"Please stop," she mumbled, but he thrashed even harder. Within seconds, he'd finished and rolled over to his side of the bed.

Lying on her back with tears streaming down the sides of her face, she rolled onto her side, slid out of bed, and crept to the bathroom shutting the door behind her.

She massaged her lower abdominal area as she sat down on the toilet; it burned when she urinated. Locking her jaw, she released and took in several deep breaths. She stood to flush and noticed blood, not a huge amount but she was bleeding. After her surgery, she wasn't able to menstruate. *He must have ripped the tissue inside*, she thought.

Flushing the toilet, she looked into the mirror; the same image she'd seen earlier in Kayla's mirror appeared.

Sometimes she felt as if there was someone else in her body. She was always talking to herself and even beginning to answer her own questions. There were times when she didn't even realize she was doing it and would jerk out of it, as if waking from a trance.

Turning around, she opened the door and stared at the person lying in their bed. Sometimes she wondered who he was and where he came from. It wasn't the Jim she married years ago. That man left when Kayla turned two and it didn't look like he'd be back anytime soon. He never used to yell at her, cut her down, or make her feel like she was nothing.

She could handle the slaps and beatings from time to time, but the verbal abuse was creating a monster inside of her and she knew one day it would surface.

****

Beep. Beep. Beep.

The alarm blared waking Clare; she pushed the snooze button before sitting up and stretching. She looked over her shoulder and saw Jim sleeping; the sound of the alarm never seemed to wake him. Sliding off the bed until her feet hit the floor, she turned off the alarm and walked into the kitchen, shutting the door behind her and poured a cup of coffee.

The sun began to break across the horizon as she sat outside with her drink. This was her morning ritual before getting Kayla up for daycare and heading out to clean houses. It helped her relax before jumping into her work, which seemed to be all she ever did these days.

Remembering the night before, she knew she wouldn't confront him about the rough intercourse or his drinking: it was a never-ending problem. She wished and prayed that she could just be okay with it, but his actions weren't easy to overcome. It's one thing to be a social drinker and another to be a drunk.

Most nights when he drank, and even when he didn't, he'd force himself upon her when she was asleep. She'd lie there pretending to enjoy it while making the sounds that he wanted to hear until he'd finished and gone to sleep. She hated doing that, but she was too tired to enjoy sex and the thought of him being with other women made her nauseous.

Stretching one last time, she went inside and got dressed. She always wore a pair of tan shorts and a white tank top. She decided to wear white because black showed the bleach splatters and it didn't look professional. Pulling her hair into a ponytail as usual, she finished and approached Jim to ask what time he would get up to look for a new job.

"What do you want?" he said, moaning.

"Just wondered what time you'd like to be up today?"

"I don't know. Just leave me alone." He rolled over to his side and threw the covers over his head. Clare turned and walked out of the room. She did not want his shit right now. She was glad to have so many clients; it was better than hanging around with him all day.

Clare gathered Kayla's belongings and kneeled beside her bed to kiss her on the forehead.

"Morning, sweetheart, how did you sleep?" Kayla smiled up at her and wrapped her arms around her neck.

"I slept good, Mommy, but I missed you."

"You missed me? Well, I missed you too, sweetie."

Kayla climbed out of bed and dressed in the outfit her mom chose for her.

Dark blue shorts with a purple button-up shirt. The daycare preferred the children wore uniforms since they would need to when they started school. Besides, Clare would rather she get those clothes dirty instead of her everyday clothing.

Clare slipped into the kitchen, poured Kayla a bowl of Lucky Charms, and set it on the table. She headed into the bedroom but didn't see Jim. Knocking on the bathroom door, she heard him grumble, "Yeah?"

"Is everything okay in there?" She turned the knob and saw him lying on the floor.

"What's wrong? Are you okay, Jim?" But knowing he wasn't by the smell of vomit coming from the toilet. She reached over him and flushed it.

"I don't feel good, Clare, I think I have the flu."

"No, it's not the flu. It's your body rejecting the booze you drank last night," she mumbled under her breath but loud enough for him to hear.

"I'm sorry, Clare, I won't do it anymore. I promise." Leaving him on the floor, she entered the kitchen and thought, *promises, promises.*

Kayla sat eating her cereal while Clare wrote Jim a note. She was glad he was fired from his job, so she didn't have to call in sick for him and lie. Besides, she was good at cleaning up his messes — whether it was right or wrong, for her it was a habit.

After dropping Kayla off, she drove to her first job of the day. She had four scheduled, but ended up getting an urgent call from a new client who needed her that afternoon. She'd have to move faster and still do a good job to fit everyone in today. She didn't want to turn anyone away; she couldn't say no because they needed whatever extra money she could make right now.

She knew how many hours it would take just by walking around the house. Most of her work took about three hours per home, but some only took two and a half hours depending on where they were located. In the summer, it didn't take as long to drive, but when the winter season came there were more people on the road. She learned new routes that had less traffic and not as many lights.

After meeting her new client that afternoon, she decided to seek help with Jim's drinking. She always made it a point not to discuss her personal matters, but when she started talking to her new client, it was like the woman could read her. There was an instant bond the moment they met.

Marie had a husband who drank himself stupid and took it out on her. Marie told her of a place that would help her deal with the emotions she had.

"You are a co-dependent," she told her. "You like to fix his problems instead of him facing them. You need to step back and let him fight the demons on his own. Stop cleaning up his mess. You can still care for him, but don't help him. Only he can help himself."

Clare needed to think only of her and Kayla, not Jim. She knew it wouldn't be easy, but she would have to pull away from him when he drank.

She called the number on her way home and wrote down the times and days of the speakers. Looking at her calendar, with all her cleanings, she chose Tuesdays at 6:30 p.m. The head speaker said she could bring her daughter if she didn't have anyone to watch her, but Clare hoped Jim would look after Kayla while she went to the meeting. If not, she'd have to ask Grammy or Brenda.

Arriving home at just past 6:00 p.m., she saw a man to her left working on his motorcycle. He looked up at her and came over. Clare pretended that she was busy doing something as he approached.

"Hi, are you Jim's wife?" he asked while wiping the grease from his hands on a rag.

"Yes, I am," she said as she helped Kayla out of the car.

"Mommy, can I go play while you talk to the man?" Kayla begged, already moving towards the play area.

"Yes, sweetie, go play for a while." Clare closed the car door and leaned against it.

"Do you live here? I've never seen you around," she asked, turning her face from the sun.

"I moved here a couple of months ago. My name's Dan, Dan McMinlow, I live on the second floor under you and your husband. He came over to my place last night and introduced himself, mostly by drinking all my beer."

"Oh, so you're the one who got him drunk. Great, now he'll always be at your place drinking."

"What? Why would you say that?"

Clare took a long look at him. She could see how fit he looked in his jeans and Harley shirt. His blond hair was short like a buzz cut and he had the bluest eyes she'd ever seen. Butterflies swirled in her stomach. She turned away. "Oh, nothing. You'll find out soon enough, I'm sure. Just be careful around him when he drinks."

Looking puzzled, he responded, "Okay, I will. We're supposed to be going for a ride on our bikes tonight. Have you seen him?"

She wasn't sure if she should answer that question with the truth. "I just got home, so I haven't been upstairs yet. His truck's here, so he's probably upstairs watching television or sleeping at a guess." Shifting the bag of rags in her hand, she called out to Kayla that it was time to go up. Looking back at Dan, she added, "I need to get going. I'll send him down."

"Thanks, it was nice to meet you."

"My name is Clare, by the way. You don't have to identify me as Jim's wife." She turned and shuffled Kayla in front of her and checked the mail before going up. Something inside didn't feel right; something was telling her that Dan McMinlow was bad news. She wasn't one to trust people and since last night's episode, Dan was on the top of her **'do not trust list'**.

Twelve

Present time…

I waited for him to leave that night before entering where she lived. The door made a click as it shut. It was dark inside her home, no lights but those from the parking lot shining through the blinds. There were only the sounds of her breathing in the next room.

Taking soft steps, I made my way to her. I placed the duct tape quickly over her mouth; she didn't even try to let out a scream or fight. It was like she knew I'd come for her. I pressed the knife under her left breast. Her eyes were fixed on mine as I continued to end her pitiful life. I was careful not to have the blood splatter on the walls, or on me. I didn't stop until I was satisfied. Watching her, I waited for the life to drain out of her.

I folded the blanket over her body, dragged her to the door, and placed her in a plastic bag, like the one they use to transfer a body to the morgue.

I looked outside into the hallway before moving her; it was late, no one was awake at that hour. After I had finished cleaning up, I closed the door behind me and lifted the plastic bag as I climbed into the elevator.

I drove down the road contemplating where to bury her body. I always enjoyed the beach and thought that would be a wonderful place to remember her. I pulled onto a dark and secluded side road and backed my vehicle in. I scouted out the beach. No one was there, not at this time of night.

Retrieving a shovel from my trunk, I carried her lifeless body and buried her. It didn't take me long to dig the hole, not with the sound of the waves crashing behind me like music. I made sure the hole was far enough away from the water and near the grass line. You know, so the water wouldn't wash the sand away and make her visible. I rolled her body into the hole and began to cover her.

When I was done, I turned to face the water and sat down. I closed my eyes and listened to the sound of the waves against the sand. The adrenaline I had felt left my body. Satisfied, I stood and went back to my vehicle. I drove to where I was staying and crawled back into my bed. It didn't take long before sleep arrived; not after the good, I had just done.

"So, you feel no remorse for what you did?" the lady asked.

"No, should I?"

"It would definitely be a start toward getting better and possibly getting out of here."

"Why would I want to leave this place?"

"Just thought you'd want to get your life back and see Clare again?"

"Clare." Her name hung in the air. "I can't change who I am and what I've done. She deserves a happy life — one without that…that asshole."

Thirteen

Detective Parks – Chicago

Detective Terry Parks had been working nonstop since his vacation to Florida a year ago. His parents had come up for the summer and left before Christmas to stay at their house in Naples. Before they left, he told his father he'd consider his offer to work in the family business, but he had to think about it before giving him an answer. Truthfully, he had only offered that consideration to get his dad off his back. He'd gone out on a few dates, but they always ended before they started. He wasn't sure why the women he met had problems with him being a detective.

He cut the engine and entered the police station.

"Hey, Terry, you got a minute?" the chief asked.

"Sure, what do you need?" He strolled into the chief's office and closed the door behind him.

"You know that case you helped out with in Ohio?"

"Yeah, what about it?" He slumped down in the chair.

"Were you ever able to solve the case?"

"No, there were too many loose ends. Missing evidence, you know how it is."

"Sure, sure, another unsolved murder."

"Is there a problem?"

"No, of course not." The chief waved is hand.

"So, what did you need to talk to me about?"

"Just dotting the i's and crossing the t's. So, do you have any new leads on the case you're working on now?"

"After getting access with the warrant you got for me, I found all the stolen merchandise hidden in her closet."

"So, she lied about the break-in to claim insurance money?"

"Yep, I arrested her yesterday. She'll be serving time in jail for quite a while."

"Good job, Terry. I knew I could count on you."

"Thanks, Chief."

"You going anywhere this year for a vacation?"

"Wasn't planning on it. Thought I'd stay here and work."

"If that's what you want," the chief laughed. "I think you work too much. You should go to Florida and visit your folks for a while."

"I'd rather work on a case."

"Your father getting on at you again about quitting?"

"Yeah, he doesn't seem to let it go."

"He just wants the best for you. You can't work your life away. You need to meet a nice woman and settle down."

"So, I hear," he replied and then stood up. "Got work to do, boss." He strode to the door and headed to his desk by the wall. First his dad and now his boss wanting him to get a life. When was the nagging going to stop?

Fourteen

Clare

She entered the condominium as Jim had finished freshening up in the bathroom. He turned off the light and strolled into the kitchen wearing jeans and a leather coat. She remembered he'd bought the coat in Ohio when he had the other motorcycle, a Honda. He put on the riding boots he'd purchased when he brought home his new Harley.

"Feeling better, I see." Her eyes glared at him.

"I slept for a while and then got up. Dan, the guy from downstairs, invited me to go riding with him. That's okay with you, isn't it?"

Not wanting to tell him what she really thought, or felt for that matter, she said, "Why would it matter what I think? You're going to do what you want anyway." She surprised herself when the words came out, but she tried to not let her feelings show.

"What's your problem?" He finished tying his boot, stood up, and zipped his coat.

"Nothing, just leave. We'll talk later when you get home." She didn't want to talk to him later or be around him. Looking at him, so smug, what she wanted to do was lash out at him. She felt something boiling inside. At any moment she could explode like fireworks on the Fourth of July, but she turned and threw the bag of rags into the washer and started the machine, hoping he'd leave and never come back. She just wanted to be alone, with Kayla.

Jim took his sunglasses and strutted out of the door, shutting it behind him.

"Finally," she muttered and went into the kitchen to cook for her and Kayla.

After putting Kayla to bed, Clare called her friend Angel in Ohio. They had worked together at the factory. Clare had meant to keep in touch with Angel when she moved, but life always seemed to get in the way.

"Hi, girlfriend," Clare said. "How are you doing?"

"Hi, Clare. It's been a while since we talked. I'm doing well. How about you? How is Florida?"

"Good, I guess. So much has happened here, I'm not sure where to start."

"What do you mean? Is everything okay?"

"For the most part, yes, but it's nice to hear your voice again." Clare sat down outside.

"You know you can talk to me about anything. Is Jim still drinking?"

"Yeah, he stops and starts, but when he starts up again, things get worse. I don't know how much longer I can take his crap, Angel. He's been sleeping around again, just like up in Ohio. I don't know what to do. I don't know how much more I can tolerate."

"Oh, sweetie, I'm sorry. Tell me. You know I'm a good listener."

"Thanks, I need a friend to lean on and who better than you?" Clare filled her in on all the events since they'd arrived in Florida, focusing on what Jim had been doing.

"Is there anything I can do?"

"I wish there was, but just being able to talk to you and hear your voice is enough, it makes me feel better."

"I'm always here for you. Maybe I can come down for a visit. I'm in need of a vacation."

"That sounds awesome. I'd love to have you here. I could show you around Naples and we can go to the beach."

"That sounds wonderful. I'll put in a request and get back to you. But for now, I need to sign off here. I transferred back to the nightshift, so I start at 10:00 p.m. and work until 7:00 a.m."

"Couldn't handle working day turn?"

"It was all right for a couple of months after you left, but I'd rather work nights."

"I sure don't miss those hours. I like being able to sleep at night, but I won't keep you. I promise to call you soon and pray you can come down."

"I'll keep in touch too. Call me anytime, sweetie."

Clare hung up the phone before turning in for the night.

****

She heard a loud rumbling that came from a motorcycle and jumped out of bed. She looked beside her and no Jim. She glanced at the clock, it was 2:00 a.m., and he wasn't home. Opening the slider, she saw it was Dan from downstairs. He was opening the garage door and pushing his bike inside. After closing the door, he looked up and saw Clare watching him.

"Where's Jim?" she called down to him, trying not to wake the neighbors.

"I'm sorry, Clare." He put his head down.

Then a taxi pulled up and her husband fell into the garage door as he stumbled out. She couldn't believe what she was seeing. He was drunk off his ass again. So much for his promises.

Discouraged, she watched him while her heart beat like a freight train. She knew he'd be loud and obnoxious once he got upstairs. Jim staggered to his feet with the help from his new friend. Clare closed Kayla's door before opening the front door.

Pushing his way through, Jim braced himself against the wall and knocked the lamp over as he made his way to the sofa.

"I can't believe you're sleeping with him!" Jim shouted at Clare.

"What are you talking about? I just met him yesterday afternoon in the parking lot downstairs." She shook her head.

"He's been this way all night, accusing me of sleeping with you," Dan said, as he stood near the door looking to make a quick exit.

"I warned you about his behavior when he drinks."

Dan stood looking at her husband on the sofa. All of a sudden, Jim leaped up and started to wrestle with Dan and they fell to the floor.

When they began rolling and pushing at each other, Clare jumped in and tried to stop them. As she tried to pull Jim off Dan, her foot caught one of their legs and she stumbled into the bookshelf, knocking over some knick-knacks on the top shelf. She tried to catch them as they fell off, but they hit her husband on the head in the process. They stopped fighting and sat upright on the floor, staring at each other.

"We never slept together, Jim. She's right we just met yesterday. I don't know why you think we are." Dan stood and fixed his shirt, while Jim sat on the floor leaning against the rose sofa.

"I know you haven't. I don't know why I think like that. Sorry, it won't happen again."

"Sure, no problem." Dan replied, rolling his eyes. "I'm going now, it's pretty late. See you around."

Jim jumped up off the floor and ran to the bathroom, Clare trotted behind him. She bolted back out when he started to vomit in the toilet.

"Sorry, Dan, you don't have to stay, I'm used to taking care of him when he gets like this."

"No, I'm sorry. We shouldn't have stopped off at the bar. Then he wouldn't be drunk." Reaching out his hand, he touched her arm.

She couldn't remember when she'd last felt a touch so gentle and by another man. Shaking the thoughts from her head, she reached for the knob and opened the door. "Thanks for helping out tonight."

"Sure, call me and let me know how he's doing."

"I don't have your number."

"I'll call your cell so you can save it."

"Sure, okay, thanks." She went to her purse, pulled out a business card, and handed it to Dan.

"See you later." She shut the door and a few seconds later she heard her phone ring twice and then stop. She glanced at it and saved the number. After shutting the lights off in the kitchen, she went into the bedroom to check on Jim.

He was lying on the floor near the toilet. After turning the light off, she climbed back into bed hoping to get some sleep. When she woke several hours later, Jim was lying next to her in bed still in the clothes he wore last night. Throwing the blankets on him, she slipped out of bed to start her morning.

****

In the weeks that followed, Jim continued to drink and each time he drank, he'd be vomiting hours later. Clare tried to tell him that he was killing himself, but he didn't want to hear what she had to say. He'd raise his hand in front of her without a word, so she knew to stop talking to him about it.

Ever since he lost his job, he had been sitting around the house and hanging around with Dan downstairs. Clare felt helpless and hopeless so she decided to start going to the meetings she should have gone to weeks ago.

Talking to Jim about it, he agreed that she needed help and promised to watch Kayla while she attended Al-Anon. She looked at her schedule for the day and wrote the meeting in for 6:30 p.m. She knew she'd be able to come home first and make dinner before catching the meeting.

Dropping Kayla off at daycare, she made her rounds and before she knew it, she was picking her daughter up. She rushed home, cooked dinner, and showered before leaving. Jim told her they would be fishing at the lake by the condo.

She entered the parking lot at the church where the meeting was being held and parked the car. Feeling nervous, she sat and stared out of the window. She didn't know what to expect, but she wanted to keep an open mind.

Stepping out of the car, she walked to the door. Once inside, she saw a door to her right. She peeked inside and saw two rows of pews, but no people. Down a hallway to the left, she saw two doors but didn't hear any sound. Turning to the right, she followed the sound of voices coming from inside the last room on the left.

Feeling her stomach turn, she made her way inside and sat down. She had a quick glance around the room and then took a few of the papers set out on the table. She shuffled through them, stopping when she saw the word 'co-dependent.' She remembered Marie saying she was a co-dependent. She opened up the pamphlet and began to read:

Codependency is a dysfunctional pattern of living and problem-solving with an alcoholic and drug abuser.

Signs of codependency are:

Maladaptive—inability to develop behavior which gets needs met.

Compulsive—psychological state in which a person acts against his or her own will or conscious desires. People who are perhaps unreliable, emotionally unavailable or needy, can be a co-dependent person trying to provide and control everything within the relationship without addressing their own needs or desires: setting themselves up for continued failure.

What are some of the symptoms of codependency?

Controlling behavior, distrust, perfectionism, avoidance of feelings, intimacy problems,

caretaking behavior, hyper vigilance (a heightened awareness for potential threat/danger), or physical illness related to stress.

Everything Clare read hit her like a bullet. She could relate to all of it. She continued through the pamphlet until the last of the group arrived.

She checked the room, studying the people in the group and the way they presented themselves when they spoke.

A brunette stood and introduced herself by first name only. She was the chairperson of Al-Anon and knew the subject well. She said they would go around the room and have each person state his or her name and why they were there.

Clare listened as the only man in the group said his name and the reason why he was there. Several other people spoke and before she knew it, it was her turn to speak. She didn't want to cry like the others, but she knew how fragile she could get.

"Hi, my name is Clare and I am here because my husband is an alcoholic." She explained their relationship and how she felt it was affecting her. When she spoke about what he'd done, she began to cry. This was the first time she'd talked about what Jim did to her besides confiding in Brenda and Angel, but she didn't always tell them everything that went on behind closed doors, as she didn't want them to feel sorry for her.

Taking a Kleenex, she wiped the tears that rolled down her cheeks. By the time everyone had spoken about their life, Clare didn't feel alone anymore. Other people were experiencing the same despair and endless pain she was. They spent time reading a book about the twelve steps to take toward a better life. Clare remembered seeing the twelve steps in an AA book that Jim had brought home. She'd even sat and read some of it just to get an idea of what recovery was all about.

She bought a couple of books about co-dependency to read at home and in between clients. People wanted to help her through the hard times and they exchanged phone numbers, saying she could call whenever she needed. The meeting ended half an hour later. Feeling a higher power inside herself, she sat and chatted with some of the women in the group before leaving.

On the way home, she replayed the meeting in her mind and what she'd read in the pamphlet.

She realized she had to work at being a better person and not let Jim's moods and drinking get the best of her.

She had the right to be happy and didn't need to try to control the situation every time he drank.

Going to this meeting showed her that she couldn't control what he did and how he acted. He was the one who decided to pick up a drink and act irrationally to her and the people around him. If he wanted to change, then it was something he had to do on his own.

She couldn't remember when she'd turned into the person she had become. Was it when he picked up the first drink three years ago? She couldn't believe how fast the years had sped by. All the times she tried to make him happy but neglected herself. It *was* okay if she wanted to sit and relax, instead of buzzing around their condo cleaning, cooking, and taking care of Jim.

After today she decided she wouldn't let the situations that developed, get to her anymore. She'd try not to control his behavior, or anyone's for that matter. She'd have to make an effort and continue to go to the meetings once a week.

****

After pulling into the parking lot, she exited the car and saw Jim with Kayla by the lake. They waved to her as she hurried over to see if they had caught anything. When she came around the corner, she noticed Dan was fishing with them. She told herself not to overreact and that they were just fishing together. Besides, she hoped that Jim wouldn't drink when he was watching their daughter.

"How's the fishing going?" she asked, looking at Dan and back to her husband.

"We only caught a few, nothing big enough to keep. Not that it would be edible anyway," Jim said, reeling in his line and casting out once more.

"Mommy, Mommy, you're home!" Kayla shouted as she ran into her mom's arms, as Clare kissed her on the cheek. "Come, I got to show you something." Clare set her down and she ran to a small sand pile near the water. "Look at what I found, Mommy," Kayla stood pointing to a stack of rocks.

"Those are beautiful, sweetie. What are you going to do with them?"

"Can I keep them, Mommy?" Looking up, she squinted in the glare of the sun that was slowing descending behind the trees.

"Maybe a few of them, but not all." Kayla bent down and picked through the rocks, gathering the ones she liked the most. Some of the rocks had sparkles that glistened when the sun hit them.

Clare sat down near Kayla and watched Jim fish. She wanted to work things out with him, but she knew it took two to make a marriage work.

She hoped that when they talked later, he'd see things her way for a change and take it upon himself to get the help he needed. She thought over what she'd say to him when they got upstairs; she knew it wasn't going to be easy to change what they'd turned into these past few years, but wasn't their love for one another worth the fight? All she knew was she didn't want their marriage to end and that it was worth fighting for.

An hour later, Clare decided to take Kayla upstairs to get her ready for bed. It was now nearly 9:00 p.m. and getting dark.

As they sat in the living room, Jim broke the silence. "We need to talk about something." He turned off the television.

Clare's stomach turned, thinking of the worst. She cleared her throat. "Sure, I wanted to talk to you about something too. You first," she said.

"I have decided since you are finally getting help that I would do the same. I'm going to start going to AA meetings again, beginning tomorrow. I think if we both start working on ourselves then we can make our relationship better and we won't argue like we do. I realize I have been an ass to you and that I need to quit drinking and help more around the house. It isn't right that you're trying to make yourself better and I keep drinking."

Clare didn't know if she heard him correctly, that he was thinking the same as she was. Her eyes lit up and a spark heated her inside.

"Clare, did you hear me?"

She nodded her head and the tears streamed down her cheeks. "You've just said what I've been thinking since I went to my meeting tonight. I don't want to fight anymore, I love you, Jim, and I always will."

"Always and forever," he said, smiling at her. He reached out and wiped her tears, then kissed her on the lips. She fell into his arms as they continued to kiss. They moved into the bedroom where they spent the rest of the night in each other's arms.

Fifteen

Clare

Sitting in her car, she'd spent the past hour looking over her cleaning schedule. Her parents were coming down to Clearwater, Florida to drive Clare's grandparents back up north. They wanted to spend some time with Kayla and her before they left. She marked her calendar for the weekend of May 12th. She'd drive up to her grandparents' house and stay for the weekend.

She couldn't believe how fast time was passing. She'd been working ten hours a day, seven days a week cleaning. She needed to get away.

Jim had landed a job working with Papa Benny at a gated community near Marco Island. Papa Benny changed jobs as much as Jim did, but Clare was glad he'd hired him as a maintenance worker. Jim was going to AA on a regular basis and seemed to be doing better this time around.

It was now the end of April and she couldn't believe how much better Jim had been since January. He was working on their marriage and was always in a great mood. She heard her phone ring and she snapped out of her thoughts.

"Hello."

"Hey, sweetie. Was just calling to see if all of you wanted to come for dinner tonight at our place," Grammy said.

Consulting her schedule, she answered, "Sure, that sounds great. What time do you want us to come?"

"Between 5:00 p.m. and 6:00 p.m. should be fine."

"Great, see you then. Oh, wait, did you talk to Jim about it yet, or do you want me to call and tell him?"

"Papa Benny said he'd let him know."

"Okay, thanks. See you later, Mom." Clare closed her cell phone and put the car in drive. She had two more clients left for the day and it was almost noon. The last cleaning would only take two and half hours, so she'd be able to pick up Kayla and head over to Grammy's house by 5:30 p.m.

****

Pulling alongside the road across from Grammy's house, she saw Jim's motorcycle sitting in the driveway. He used to call her throughout the day, but for the last couple of weeks he told her he was too busy with work and then AA. She didn't want to fight so she let it go.

Ringing the doorbell, she heard Grammy say it was open. They lived in a townhouse off Pine Ridge near I-75. Half of the homes were townhouses, and the others were condo apartments and houses. They lived upstairs and their neighbor lived downstairs. In front were two sets of garage doors, one for each resident.

After removing her shoes, Kayla raced up the stairs to see her Grammy. Clare sat on the step to untie her shoes and set them to the side. Exhausted, she held the railing and climbed the stairs.

Clare said hello and hugged Grammy and Papa Benny, her eyes scanning the room for Jim. She spotted him sitting on the lanai talking on the phone. Making her way outside, she sat down next to him. When he saw her, he quickly hung up the phone.

"Hey, Clare, you made it." Looking nervous, he shoved his cell phone into his pocket.

"Who were you speaking with on the phone?"

"Oh, just my sponsor from AA." He reached over and kissed her on the cheek.

Something was wrong. He always talked on the phone with his sponsor. Why would this time be any different? He was hiding something from her but acting as if everything was peachy. *Maybe I'm just assuming things again,* she thought.

Three hours later, they were gathering their things and heading home for the night. Stepping outside, Clare noted the air was cooler than normal so she slid on her jacket and carried Kayla to the car. "Where's your leather coat?" she asked Jim who was climbing on his motorcycle.

"Oh, I forgot it at my sponsor's house. I'll pick it up tomorrow when I see him at AA."

"Are you coming home?"

"Yeah, I'll see you there." Jim straddled his bike and drove away.

****

On the drive home, Clare didn't see Jim anywhere. *Maybe he's home already and waiting for us*, she thought. Turning into the parking lot, she noticed there were no lights on upstairs. Looking around she didn't see him anywhere. She scooped Kayla into her arms and climbed the three floors to their home. After turning on the lights, she put Kayla to bed and closed the door. She changed into her pajamas, but Jim still wasn't home. Feeling anxious, she paced back and forth in the living room. She sat out on the balcony and spotted a single headlight appearing in the distance. She watched and listened as a motorcycle glided through the parking lot. She could tell by the sound that it was Jim's.

He stopped at the garage door and opened it. Clare's heart raced when she noticed he was wearing his leather coat. In the back of her mind she thought about the conversation they had earlier. She remembered him telling her that he'd left it at his sponsor's place, but she knew he was lying to her.

She stood up and went back inside to wait for him. Moments later, Jim came through the door while Clare pretended to be busy in the kitchen. Without looking up, she asked, "Who is she, Jim? I know you are seeing someone, so who is it?"

"I don't know what you're talking about, Clare," he replied while sitting on the couch to remove his boots.

"I'm not stupid. You didn't have your leather coat earlier, so where does she live? Did you meet her at AA?"

"Just leave it alone, Clare. I've never given you any indication that I was with another woman."

"Maybe you didn't come right out and say it, but the phone call you ended earlier was suspicious and then saying your jacket was at your sponsors' house. You know, all I have to do is call him and ask if you were just there. I know who your sponsor is remember? You introduced us at the Super Bowl party in February." She could tell by the look on his face that she was right.

163

"Okay, okay, I left it at a woman's house, someone I go to AA with. It's no big deal. We're just friends," he barked as he set his boots by the front door.

He thinks he's so sly. I can't believe he'd do this to me again, she thought while holding back the tears. *I should have noticed.* She thought back over the past couple of weeks and there was something she didn't pay much attention to at the time, but it came rushing back to her. *I didn't think anything of it when he was pulling away and not being affectionate toward me. Jim has wanted sex almost every night but for the past two weeks, he hasn't. I should've seen it coming but I was so tired from work.*

She wiped away the tears rolling down her face before Jim came back into the living room. This is my fault if he leaves. How will I pay the rent and support Kayla? How will I make it on my own? Anger surfaced but then subsided; she took in a deep breath and locked up her emotions inside. She didn't want to hurt anymore — she just wanted things to be the way they were years ago, but she knew that it most likely wouldn't happen. They were losing each other, and he didn't want her anymore.

They hadn't gone out as a couple since Kayla was born, but his drinking had played a factor.

Clare was afraid that he'd get drunk then act crazy and stupid. He always told her that she was no fun anymore and that she didn't participate when they had sex. How could she after the way he treated her and being unfaithful?

Maybe I'd be better off without him. I can make it on my own with Kayla. I am strong. I don't need him. I have a great job and I make enough money. Who needs that asshole anyway? Let him leave. She's the one who will have to live with him, not me. Feeling more confident, she turned off the lights.

She decided before closing her eyes that it was time to come up with a plan to take care of herself and Kayla. She knew she'd have to start putting money aside and make a way out.

She spent the next week finding an attorney. She wanted one that would give her a free consultation so she could see how much a divorce would cost.

The next day she spent her lunch break writing down the bills she paid each month and how much she could afford to pay for a place of her own, including the car payment, electric, and rent costs. She kept a positive attitude and reminded herself that she could make it without him, but would have to stay with him until she had enough money saved to rent a place of her own.

Jim was relaxing on the sofa when Clare came home with Kayla. She put the groceries away and started dinner.

"We need to talk, Clare, it's important," Jim said without looking up from the television.

"Sure, what do you want to talk about?"

"I want a divorce."

Not sure if she'd heard him right, she continued to chop vegetables for dinner. "Does this have to do with that woman from AA?"

"Yes and no. She told me that she couldn't be with me if I was still married to you. That's the yes. And no because let's face it, Clare, we aren't the same people we used to be."

What he was saying was true, but he had never come right out and asked for a divorce before.

"Did you hear me? I said I want a divorce."

"Yes, Jim, I heard you. I'll get an attorney and give you what you want. Jim always gets what he wants."

"Don't get pissed at me. You know things haven't been good between us."

"Yeah, but I wonder whose fault *that* is. I know you'll try to blame me for what happened in Ohio, but that's done and over with. I haven't done anything to make you cheat on me or make you drink. You did that yourself, Jim. I can't believe I could love someone like you. Do you remember our vows? Because I do and I think about that day all the time, but I guess you have forgotten, what a marriage is or just don't give a shit. Do what you want. If you think life will be better without Kayla and me then fine, get out of here, because we don't need you anymore. You want to know something, Jim? You can't make it without me. I do everything for you. So go, get out of this house and be with this other woman, I don't care."

The words shot out of her mouth without her registering what she was saying to him. She needed to save money first before they went their separate ways, but that wasn't going to happen if she kept this up. Jim didn't even question what she said to him; he just stared at her.

Finishing up in the kitchen, she checked on Kayla before heading off to bed. It was hard to sleep that night; she kept replaying in her mind what she'd said to Jim. Although she meant every word, she couldn't believe she'd told him how she felt. It was one thing to feel a certain way and another to let the person know how you felt.

She was becoming bitter, angry, and sad all at the same time. Depression was sinking in and she knew she couldn't live a life with him much longer. Besides, she didn't want Kayla growing up in a house where her parents argued and didn't love each other. She also didn't want her to see Jim when he drank; not when she thought the world of her dad.

Clare's heart broke every time she thought of her daughter and what she'd think of her if they left, but she knew she shouldn't stay—if not for Kayla, then for herself. They deserved a better life, a life without a drunk. With someone who would love them, take care of them and never lay a hand on her again. Not someone who would call her names and downgrade her, but the future didn't look as bright as Clare dreamed it would be. Of course, all the dreams she once had were never going to come true. The promises he had continued to give her were just words. Nothing more.

As she lay in bed trying to quiet her mind, she didn't even notice he wasn't in bed with her that night.

Sixteen

Clare

The next morning Clare made an appointment to meet an attorney. She'd find out if she should be worried about Jim taking Kayla from her. She knew he'd do it just to get back at her.

Entering the front door, she saw two elevators on the right side next to a door that led to the stairs. On the wall by the elevators hung a map behind a sheet of framed glass, which outlined all the rooms with the names of the people who occupied them.

She spotted his name, Attorney Kirk Gabble: Room 314A. Stepping towards the elevators, she pushed the up button and waited. The elevator dinged as it came to a halt. She entered and pushed the button for the third floor. Her stomach tightened and her hands trembled as she waited in the office for the attorney to call her in. She wasn't sure if she could go through with the meeting, but she knew she had to find out what it would cost for a divorce and what she could do to protect Kayla and her.

She had three attorneys to choose from, but she went with the one that publicized a free consultation. She glanced up every few seconds while flipping through a magazine.

"Clare Culback," the receptionist said. "He can see you now."

After tossing the magazine on the table in front of her, she stood and followed the young woman with black curly hair. Walking into the consultation room, she saw he had a few diplomas on the wall. On his desk sat several picture frames, which she assumed were of his family, and mounds of manila folders with people's names listed on them.

She pulled the chair out and took a seat, setting her purse in her lap.

"So, what brings you in today, Mrs. Culback?" Attorney Gabble asked. His thin brown hair accentuated his blue eyes and freckled face. He didn't look much older than thirty.

She cleared her throat. "I'm here because my husband asked for a divorce."

"How do you feel about him wanting a divorce?"

"I know why he wants one, but I'm afraid."

"What scares you, Mrs. Culback? Did he do or say anything threatening?"

"He's said that if I ever leave him, he'll make it so I don't see our daughter again. I know he is seeing someone else too."

"Do you have proof of that?"

"Only what he has told me and the way he has been acting lately."

"How many children do you have?"

"One."

"Do you own anything, like a house or cars?"

"We rent and the car is in my name but the truck is in his. The only other possession we have is the furniture in our condo. There are no big bank accounts or anything worth fighting over."

"I see. It will be pretty easy then."

Clearing her throat again before answering, "What about my daughter?"

"First, I want you to tell me about your husband. What is he like as a father and a husband?"

"He doesn't spend much time with her, if that's what you're asking. As a husband, well, he's…he's a drunk. He goes on rampages. One day he'll drink and go ballistic, and then a week later he's fine. It's like he has high highs and low lows. He's tried several times to kill himself with guns, knives, and pills. I wouldn't say he actually tried to kill himself, but he does say he's going to and then he end up

171

calling the cops. They come to the house and put him in an institution for a few weeks, like a detox of some sort. He's had six DUIs and has spent time in jail, but nothing seems to make a difference. I'm afraid for myself and my daughter when he gets like that."

"So, he's had six DUI's in Florida?"

"No, only one here. The other five are from when we lived in Ohio."

"May I ask you a personal question, Mrs. Culback?"

"Haven't you been asking personal questions? Sorry, I don't mean to sound rude. I just become protective at times." Tears raced down her cheeks.

"That's okay, I understand. It sounds like you're a co-dependent. My question is why do you stay with him when he treats you like this?"

"Because I don't have anywhere else to go and a place of my own costs money."

"I can make sure he pays you child support, but I wouldn't suggest you stay with him if he's like what you've described. One day he could take it out on you or your daughter. I've seen many cases like this and, well, it's always best that you get out before anything happens to you or your daughter, Mrs. Culback."

She nodded and shifted in her chair. "So, how much do you think it will cost to divorce him?"

"Anywhere from twenty-five hundred to four thousand, but you don't pay all of that because he should pay half."

"He doesn't have that kind of money."

"You could always do the divorce yourself. Then it would only cost you a few hundred dollars for processing fees. The courthouse on Airport Road has all the documents you need. You fill them out, have him sign them and take them to the court to have them notarized. It may take a few months, but it will save you money in the long run."

She looked down at her purse and then up at him. "I guess I'll have to do it myself then. Sorry to waste your time." She stood up and shook his hand before leaving.

"Clare, be careful. You're sitting on a time bomb waiting to go off."

"I'll keep that in mind. Thanks again for your time." She left the office and headed outside.

Sitting in her car, she processed what he'd told her, knowing that everything he'd said to her was true, but she needed a plan before she could leave him. Another condo would cost money and that was something she didn't have, also she didn't want to ask her parents for the money. They didn't even have a clue what had been going on down here.

By the time she got home, Jim was waiting for her.

"Can we talk?" Jim asked.

Making her way into the kitchen to start dinner, she answered, "Sure, what do you want to talk about?"

"Last night I said I wanted a divorce. Do you remember that?"

"Of course. I remember it was just last night."

"Well, I've changed my mind," he said, looking down at his hands and then back up at her.

"Okay, what's happened to change your mind?" Putting her lunchbox to the side, she brought some pans out to start braising the beef she'd bought earlier for dinner.

"Nothing happened. I just changed my mind."

She began slicing vegetables and decided not to bring up the attorney.

"Also, I invited Dan from downstairs to dinner tonight, if that's okay with you?"

"Thanks for the short notice," she mumbled under her breath. She turned towards the cabinet and pulled out four plates. Jim announced he was going downstairs to tell Dan that dinner would be ready in an hour.

After Jim left, she stepped outside on the porch and thought about what could have happened that had changed his mind and why he'd invited Dan to dinner.

She decided to push the thought from her mind; it wasn't worth her time and energy to try to understand him. All she knew was, that she wasn't happy being with him. With everything he had put her through — his drinking, cheating, and lying, she just didn't feel the same about him. She was in fact starting to hate him, but she didn't know if she had the courage to leave. Why did he continue to hurt her? Was it a game to him?

"Well, I'm not playing his game anymore. Tomorrow I'm stopping at the court, picking up the papers, and leaving him no matter what it takes. I can't keep living like this. My head and heart can't take it." She spoke aloud. She knew she could figure out a way to pay for her own place; that wasn't what was bothering her. It was the fact that he'd stop at nothing to make her stay with him because he couldn't make it without her. She's the one who'd been supporting him and all his addictions.

After dinner, they sat around telling stories about embarrassing things they'd done. Clare couldn't figure out why her husband would invite Dan to dinner after accusing them of sleeping together. Sure, he was a nice guy and good-looking. She could see how solid his arms and chest were through his tight shirt. He actually made her blush when he looked at her, but Clare remembered she was married to Jim.

175

Her mind flashed back to a guy named Brent. The whole situation was all a big misunderstanding. When she worked at the factory in Ohio, she was talking to him and he sent her an email stating all the sexual things he wanted to do to her. Jim was the one who read the email first and accused Clare of sleeping with him.

Shortly after that Jim started drinking, but the truth was she had never cheated on Jim. The thought of being unfaithful never even crossed her mind. Brent was only a friend to her and someone she could talk to, but apparently, he wanted more. She wasn't a cheater and never would be. Marriage, she knew, was a commitment between two people who loved each other, no matter what.

****

That night as she lay in bed, she couldn't get Dan off her mind. When she met him, she hadn't cared for him one bit, she didn't trust him. She even blamed him for Jim's drinking, but five months had gone by since they moved here, and he seemed to be hanging around every day.

****

The following day, when she was driving to her next cleaning job, Dan called her.

176

"Hello, Dan. This is a surprise," she spluttered while turning down the radio.

"Hi, Clare. Was just thinking about you and wanted to chat."

"Sure, what's up?" Her heart beat hard through her chest. She couldn't understand why he was calling her. The feeling reminded her of the Brent situation.

"Nothing much, at work, kind of slow today. Hey, thanks for dinner last night. It's not very often I have a home-cooked meal."

"You're welcome. What kind of work do you do?"

"I work for the state. Checking meters and electrical boxes."

"That sounds cool. What made you get into that line of work?"

"I worked for the state when I lived in Ohio."

"I didn't know you were from Ohio. You didn't mention that last night. Where in Ohio?"

"Streetsboro."

"I guess the world is a small place after all. I lived one hour east of there. I bet you like it better down here. At least you can ride your motorcycle every day and not have to worry about the snow."

"Yeah, that's one of the reasons I moved. That and I was laid off from my job. So, I figured what the hell, there's nothing keeping me here."

"Do you have any brothers or sisters?"

"I have one brother. He still lives in Ohio with his wife and three daughters. Do you have any siblings?"

"I have a sister living in Ohio and she has twin boys. It's amazing how much you and I have in common and never knew it."

"I know, right. Well, I won't keep you long. Just wanted to call and say hi and thank you for last night. I had a great time."

"You're welcome and thanks for calling."

She closed her cell and smiled. She had arrived at her job ten minutes ago, but she didn't want to get off the phone.

She whipped through her next two cleaning jobs and headed to the third. Remembering the conversation earlier with Dan, she couldn't help but have a smile on her face for the rest of the day. There was something about him that intrigued her, though she couldn't quite put her finger on it.

When she talked to him, he made her feel good about herself — a feeling she hadn't had in a long time. Sure, she loved her husband, but no matter what she did, it was never good enough for him.

He was never happy with her or what she did for him. She was always thinking of him and Kayla, instead of herself.

****

Pulling into the parking lot of her home, she checked her client book for the next day's schedule. She couldn't believe that in two weeks she was going to see her parents for the first time since she'd moved to Florida. She wanted to hug them both and tell them she loved them. She missed her family and couldn't wait to see them again. It was only her and Kayla going. Jim was staying at home because of work. Besides, she needed time away to think and clear her head. Maybe then she could make sense of her situation and come to a decision about getting a divorce.

Seventeen

Clare

It was Friday. She couldn't believe how fast the last two weeks had flown by. She carried their bags downstairs and placed them in the car behind her seat. She packed Kayla's DVD player so she'd have something to do for the three-hour drive up north and a few other distractions that would occupy her on the ride.

She was looking forward to this weekend and needed the time off work. They said their goodbyes to Jim and drove away. She wasn't too keen about driving on the highway, but knew she had to get used to it if she wanted to visit her grandparents again in the fall.

The drive was stressful, but she was able to make it there by 7:00 p.m. She would've made it sooner, but she hit traffic in Tampa.

Pulling into the yard by her parents' mini-van, she turned off the car and gathered up Kayla from the back seat.

By the time she had Kayla out, Clare's mom was standing near the car waiting for a hug and kiss. Clare set Kayla down and embraced her mother, doing her best to hold back the tears.

Clare's dad helped carry in their suitcases while she said hello to her grandparents who were in the living room watching *Wheel of Fortune*.

They spent the weekend talking about everything that was going on up in Ohio and Clare filled them in on some of the people she cleaned for. She didn't want to discuss Jim but when she was alone outside with her mom, Clare ended up telling her about what he'd done in Ohio and after their arrival to Florida. She felt relieved after holding everything in for so long.

Sunday morning came too soon, and Clare knew she had to leave later that day for home. Standing outside her grandparents' house after returning from church, she checked her phone and saw that she had two messages. She listened to the first one; her heart raced, and her body trembled. It was from Dan. The other message was from Brenda. Both messages stated it was important that she call back ASAP. She dialed Brenda first.

"Hey, what's up?" She tried to sound nonchalant.

"Clare, I only called to tell you this because you are my best friend and I wouldn't hide anything from you."

"What's going on, Brenda?" she asked as she took in a deep breath.

"Last night at around 12:30 a.m., when I was at the bank depositing the money from Pizza Hut, Jim called me saying we needed to talk. I knew you were out of town, so I asked if he could just tell me over the phone, but he said he needed me to come to the condo. Clare, he sounded drunk, so I didn't want to go, but I had to know for sure before telling you all this. So, ten minutes later, I arrived, and he had a case of beer next to him by the sofa. He'd drank over half of it."

"What did he want to talk about?" She felt as if she was going to throw up and started pacing the driveway.

"He asked me if you and Dan were sleeping together. I told him you weren't and that you are just friends, but he didn't want to hear it. Anyway, I told him I was going home and he asked me if I would watch a porno movie with him. I told him no and left. I had to tell you, Clare. I'm sorry."

Clare was speechless. *He asked me to watch a porno movie with him* was all that kept replaying in her head.

"What are you going to say to him?"

"I don't know, but I'll tell you one thing. I'm not putting up with this shit anymore. That's it. I'm done. I've accepted his drinking, cheating and broken promises for three years now, but I can't and won't live this life anymore."

"If it helps, I'm moving into that two-bedroom plus den in a week or two, so you and Kayla can come live with me and we can share the rent until you get a place of your own?"

"You'd do that for me?"

"You're my best friend, Clare. I know you'd do the same for me."

"Okay, then. I'll tell him when I get home that we're moving out in two weeks."

"Sounds good. I'll keep you posted when I get settled into my new place."

"Thanks, Brenda, I appreciate you letting us stay with you."

She ended the call and dialed Dan's number. Two rings later, he answered.

"Hey Clare, I see you got my message."

"What the hell happened last night?" She was surprised by how angry she was and thought that her husband was lucky he was one hundred and eighty miles away at the moment.

"We went out for a bite to eat last night and he ordered a couple drinks. I mentioned that I thought he'd stopped drinking and was in AA, so I asked if you knew he was drinking again. He just said, "Clare's not here. She won't know." He had about three or four drinks and then we went home. I don't know what happened after that, but I thought you should know."

Clare couldn't believe what was happening. First Brenda and now Dan. She was sick and tired of what Jim was doing and realized that he wasn't going to stop drinking and cheating; it was just who he was, but her involvement needed to end.

"Thanks for letting me know, Dan, but I'll tell you what happened after you both went home." She filled him in on what Brenda had told her.

"What the hell was he thinking, Clare?"

"He doesn't think. He just does what Jim wants to do, no matter what the outcome. He doesn't care who's around or what they think about him. He's an asshole, but it's going to change when I get home. I'm going to find another place to live." Her adrenaline was pumping and she meant what she said, she had no choice. Enough was enough. She was finally going to leave him.

She ended the call, shut her phone, and stared out at the road. Her head was spinning now, but she knew what she had to do. She'd tell him how she felt and that she was leaving with Kayla.

"Everything okay, Clare?" her mom asked, joining her.

"No, everything is not okay."

Clare's mom wrapped her arms around her and held her close. "What is it, Clare? What happened?"

Pulling away, Clare looked up at her mom. "You remember what I told you this weekend?"

"Yeah, about Jim and his actions."

"I guess he thought that since I was away this weekend, that he would drink." She explained both of the calls.

"Oh, Clare, sweetie, I'm so sorry. What are you going to do?"

"Mom, it's over. I can't live like this anymore and Kayla deserves better. He's not a husband or a father to us, and I've been a fool to think he'd change. I've tried, but I just don't have the strength to do this with him. Sure, I love him but love isn't enough."

"I talked to your father last night about what you told me and if it helps, we are behind you no matter what you decide. We just want you to be happy and safe. If he is mistreating you in any way, then leave. Take Kayla and live somewhere else — be happy. We don't want him to hurt you or our granddaughter any longer."

"Thanks, Mom. I did need to hear you say that. I know I don't need anyone's permission, but it is good to know I'm not alone."

"We always worry about you and wished you hadn't moved down there, but we do understand why. We think it was more Jim than you, but I also know you love what you do for a living. Just take care of yourself. We noticed that you've lost a lot of weight since you left Ohio."

"I've been under a lot of stress. I promise I'll eat better and take care of myself and Kayla." Her entire life she'd wanted their approval and for them to love her no matter what. She just wondered if she was strong enough to make it on her own without Jim.

After they all ate lunch, Clare packed up the car, secured Kayla into her car seat, and drove back down to Naples. All she could think about was what Brenda had told her. The closer she got to home, the more upset she became. She was hoping the drive back would calm her, but it just made her more angry and bitter. She wasn't sure what she'd say to him, but why should she hold it all in? Besides, he deserved to know how she felt.

Pulling into the parking lot, she saw Jim talking to Dan inside the garage. She put the car in park and shut off the engine. She didn't even acknowledge him. She opened the back door and started to unload their luggage, then took

Kayla out of her car seat. She made her way upstairs and set their bags down by the washer and began to throw their clothes into it, she then went into the kitchen. Whenever anything was troubling her, she always kept herself busy.

"Hey, Clare. How was your weekend?"

"My weekend was great, but I should ask you how your weekend went." Before she knew it, words started flying out her mouth and by the end, the last thing she said to him was, "We're moving out in a few weeks. I'm done with your crap, Jim!"

She'd caught him off guard and he was speechless. For once, she was in control of the situation: not him. He always had an answer for everything, but he couldn't think of anything to change what she'd said. Clare started frying chicken, hoping he'd just leave and not continue their conversation. He turned and walked out to the balcony.

****

For the next two weeks, she did her best to ignore him. Although he tried several times to change her mind, she wouldn't budge. He even bought flowers for her, but she stood her ground. For once, he did chores around the house to get her attention, but that didn't work either. He was only being kind to change her mind. She knew he wouldn't continue to do everything after he had what he wanted. She had to keep her word about what she'd said to him. She was nervous about moving out, but she had to if she wanted a better life for Kayla and herself.

****

Tuesday morning was a light day for her; she had a three-hour cleaning job in the morning and then was off to an office building to clean and do some paperwork. Fred was the only client who wanted her to help with the admin instead of just cleaning. She didn't mind though as it broke up the monotony of her regular duties.

As she was packing up the car with her cleaning supplies, Fred called and canceled, telling her that he had many appointments today but he could use her on Thursday instead. She fit him into her schedule and decided to head home since he was the only client she had left for the day.

Driving down Livingston, she received a call from Brenda asking her what she was doing. She told her she was on her way home, then Brenda said she had the key to her new place and wanted Clare to see it.

Clare made a right instead of a left on Santa Barbara and turned into Clayview Estates. She followed the directions Brenda gave her over the phone and parked the car. She waved to her friend who was standing outside on the second floor of the condo complex. Once beside her,

Brenda reached out and gave her a hug, and then they walked inside. The place was furnished with beds and tables. Everything a person would need and it only cost $1000.00 a month.

"Wow, this is nice, Brenda."

"Thanks. It's plenty big enough."

With a laugh, Clare asked, "So when do I move in?"

Brenda didn't know that Clare was joking, so she replied, "What time does Jim get home? We can go get some of your things now."

Clare's face flushed and her heart raced. "Are you serious, Brenda?"

"Yeah, I'm serious! You said you'd move in with me, so let's do it!"

Before she could change her mind, they drove over to Clare's condo. Arriving in separate vehicles, they ran upstairs and started throwing her belongings in garbage bags. Clare took all her clothes, not that she had a lot living down here, and shoved them into a bag, as well as toiletries from her bathroom and toys from Kayla's room. After filling a few more bags, they stood in the foyer looking around; they had everything Clare wanted to take. The rest she would get another day when Jim wasn't home.

"What about your Elvis collectibles?"

Clare knew she couldn't keep them here with Jim. He would be pissed when he found out they weren't living there anymore. She remembered the last time he got angry and destroyed several of the Elvis memorabilia she had.

"I have some empty tubs in the garage downstairs, I'll run down and get them, and then we'll hide them in the back of the garage so he won't find them." Doing as she said, they had all of her Elvis collection packed in twenty minutes and were carrying the containers down to the garage. Clare found a spot at the back to hide them and covered them with a tarp she'd found. Looking at her cell phone, she saw it was nearly 2:00 p.m.

"Okay, let's grab the bags and we're done," Brenda announced. After taking the bags down and setting them in the car, Clare raced upstairs to lock up. She headed into the master bathroom, then the bedroom and did the same in Kayla's room, also taking more toys for her daughter.

Before closing the door to a life of broken promises and fear, she stood studying the pictures on the walls. Why couldn't he just stop drinking and cheating?

Why couldn't he just love me and be happy with me? She didn't have the answers to those questions, but hoped that one day she would.

She leaped when the clock on the wall chimed three times, so she headed out the door, locking it behind her.

Eighteen

Clare

Brenda and Clare took the bags from the car and set them in the den where Clare was going to keep their belongings. She would be sleeping in one of the twin beds next to Kayla until Brenda brought Samantha down for the summer, and after that she'd sleep in the den.

Brenda sat on the lanai while Clare put her meager possessions away. A few minutes later, Clare left to go to the grocery store. That's when the first call came through. Her cell phone rang as she held it in her hand looking at the name on the phone.

She hesitated before answering. "Hello."

"Clare," Jim said. "Please, come back! Don't leave me! I promise I will never drink again!" he pleaded.

"I can't and won't come back to you, Jim." She tried to keep her voice low. "I am sorry, but I had to leave. I can't live like that anymore. You always say you'll change but you never do. You always go back to drinking and I always get my mind fucked by you, for what, your entertainment? Not anymore, Jim. I deserve a better life, a life that isn't filled with the disaster that follows your drinking."

"I can't live without you, Clare. I need you."

"What do you need, exactly? Do you need me because you love me and want to be with me until we grow old like we have always dreamed? Or is it because I paid the bills and you never had to worry. What is it that you want from me, Jim? What you need is time to think and get help and maybe, just maybe, we can work things out in the future, but for now you need to make your life better. You need to find the man I married and bring him back; the Jim I fell in love with a long time ago." The other end of the line fell silent as she stood in the grocery store wanting to get off the phone with him. Talking to him made her stomach hurt and her hands shake from the stress and nervousness she was feeling inside. She heard him sniffling, as if he was crying. He always apologized for what he did and said while he was intoxicated, but this time she couldn't tell if he was really sorry or fooling her once again.

"I promise you, I will get help. I will prove to you that I love you more than you know and I will never hurt you again. Just give me another chance?"

"I have given you more than enough chances, Jim. I've actually lost count how many I've given you. I'm not coming back to you, not until I know you have stopped drinking for good." Although part of what she'd said was true, he'd have to prove to her that he was the man she once married before she'd think of going back to him. He'd have to stop drinking forever; that was something she knew he couldn't and wouldn't do, no matter how hard he tried.

Lying she said, "Look, I have to finish up cleaning and pick up Kayla from preschool." She didn't want him to know that she was at the grocery store. Not that he knew which store she was standing in, but he always had a way of getting information out of her.

"Okay, fine, but can I talk to you again later or tomorrow?"

"Sure, yeah, I guess. I will try to call you between clients tomorrow." The last thing she wanted to do was hurt him. Sounds stupid, but she loved him — she always had, no matter how many times he hurt her. She just couldn't be as mean to him as he'd been to her. Besides, she knew the man she met five years ago, so she still hoped that he would come back to her.

"Goodbye, Jim. I really do wish things were different, but they're not. You just have to give us time."

"Goodbye, Clare. I hope to see you soon. I love you," he replied.

She pushed the button on the phone disconnecting them and slid it in her back pocket. She didn't want to talk to him later or tomorrow, but why did he make her feel obligated to do so? Why couldn't she just do what she said and mean it? She couldn't keep telling him how she felt inside, not until he got help with his drinking.

Pushing the cart down the aisle, she chose ingredients for their dinner and then went to the checkout before leaving the store. The sun beamed down on her face, making it hard for her to see as she carried the groceries to her car. The air was dry with no wind, which made it feel hotter outside.

After putting the grocery bags into the car, she sat in the driver's seat, took several deep breaths, and fought back the tears before leaving to pick up Kayla from preschool.

Kayla hadn't asked Clare any questions, nor did she seem concerned about their new living arrangements. She seemed happy and playful as always. After they got back, she sat in the living room watching Dora the Explorer on

TV and playing with the toys Clare had brought with them.

Taking some iced tea from the refrigerator, she checked on Kayla and went out onto the lanai where Brenda was sitting. She collapsed into the chair with exhaustion.

"I finished preparing dinner for us," she said.

"Good. Life will get better for you," Brenda replied. "What do you have going on tomorrow?"

"I have an eight-hour cleaning job and then I'll pick up Kayla from preschool. Why, what's up?"

"Just thought you might want to grab a bite for lunch?"

"How about we meet for lunch on Friday? I only have two cleanings that day."

"That sounds good. What time is good for you?"

"Let's say 11:30 a.m. at the café on Airport and Immokalee? I hear they have great sandwiches."

"Sounds good. I'm glad you left him, you know. You deserve someone who will treat you better and love you for who you are. I just want you to be happy."

"I know you do and I want to be happy too. I just never thought we'd end up this way. I never thought he'd ever pick up a drink when I met him five years ago. The first two years were great, but after that, I'm not sure what changed. It just happened so fast and every day with him got worse and worse. His moods altered and I never knew when he came home if he was going to be in a good mood or a bad mood.

I always bought him whatever he wanted just to make him happy, even if it meant I had to work more jobs to make the money. The sad thing was, he'd get what he wanted, and then after a week or two it didn't make him happy anymore. He wanted something better that cost more money. I was throwing money out of the window instead of using it for something we needed. He was never good with money, so that's why I took care of the finances. It's bad enough that we lost our house in Ohio and two vehicles from bankruptcy, all because he wanted to drink and not go to work. Then we chose to move down here, I guess to run away from the problems. Boy, was that a mistake! The problems just go with you, no matter where you live. If it weren't for you having this place, I'd never have been able to leave him. I want to thank you for that, Brenda. I appreciate you letting us stay here for a while."

"You don't have to thank me, Clare, that's what friends are for and I'm sure you'd have done the same for me if it was the other way around."

197

"Yes, I would have." She inhaled the peace and quiet as the wind tousled her hair. She closed her eyes and took in a deep breath, feeling the weight lift off her shoulders.

Clare was awoken by the sound of her cell phone ringing. She sprang out of bed and trotted to the den down the hall to silence the ringer, hoping not to wake anyone up. She was half asleep when she answered.

"Hello."

"Hello, Clare." Jim replied. "What are you doing?" She unplugged the phone from the charger and sat down on the floor with her knees bent to her chest. She couldn't shake the sleepiness off as she listened to his voice on the other end. "It's 3:00 a.m. and I was sleeping. What do you think I was doing? Why are you calling me?"

"I couldn't sleep, Clare. I miss you and I need you."

"Are you drinking, Jim? I don't want to talk to you if you are. What do you want? I don't know why we can't talk later, it's too early in the morning," she stated and then yawned.

"Please, come home! Please just give me another chance. I don't want to live without you, Clare." His voice was soft and sweet.

"Jim, this isn't the time and it's only been one night. How can you miss me already?" she asked in a low whisper. "It's not like you haven't been separated from me before."

Her mind flashed back to the many times he hadn't come home when he was out drinking and had gone off with another woman. He must have thought she was an idiot and didn't know where he was or what he was doing. As her thoughts filled with hate, her stomach ached with disgust.

She couldn't believe that she'd loved this man and stayed with him for as long as she had.

"Clare, are you there?"

"Yeah, I'm still here. Look, I'm tired and I'm going back to bed. We will talk about this in the morning, okay?"

"I don't know if I'll be here in the morning. I have a gun and I'm going to kill myself. I just wanted to tell you that I love you and Kayla and I am sorry for everything."

"Jim, you are not going to kill yourself. You always say that you are or will, but the fact is you don't even have a gun, remember? The sheriff's department took them away from you the last time you did this, and I know you don't have much money to buy another one. Just go to bed and we will talk in the morning, okay?"

"You promise you'll call me?"

"I said I will, now get some sleep. I am hanging up the phone now."

"Okay, talk to you later. Always remember that I love you, Clare. Always and forever."

"Goodnight, Jim. I love you too. Talk to you later." She closed her cell phone before he could say another word and turned off the ringer. As she sat there in the dark, it registered in her head what she'd just said to him. She knew she loved him but she also hated him at the same time.

She lay beneath the covers waiting for sleep to come. She turned and stared at Kayla who was sound asleep in the next bed. *She's my life and I will do anything to keep her safe,* Clare thought. *Isn't that what moms are for, or even parents for that matter? I hope one day she doesn't hate me for leaving her dad, but I couldn't let her live in a house filled with disgust and a father who chooses drinking over us. She deserves more than that and I will do whatever it takes to protect her.*

****

The alarm blared beside her as she reached over and hit the snooze button before it beeped again. Lying there and not wanting to get out of bed, she stretched her arms above her head and turned off the alarm. She peered over at Kayla who was still asleep. She got up and strolled into the kitchen to make coffee, then staggered out onto the lanai.

As she sat sipping her drink, her mind wandered back to her conversation last night with Jim on the phone. She couldn't grasp why he just couldn't stop drinking. Why did he have to drink? Wasn't there more to life than just drinking? She used to drink when she went out with friends, but she was more of a social drinker. She never got plastered the way he did when he drank. Even in Ohio, he used to pull this shit with killing himself. She didn't believe he'd actually do it because he would have done it already.

He said he loved her, but if a man loves you then he wouldn't hurt you. Would he? She'd just answered her own question. She was living it.

After finishing her coffee, she went back inside and dressed. She had an all-day job ahead but wasn't in the mood to work. Sometimes she had to talk herself into it. She woke up Kayla and got her dressed for preschool. She had to be at her workplace by 8:30 a.m., but she was always early. Martha didn't care what time she arrived as long as she put in her eight hours of cleaning. Martha had a huge home with five bedrooms, two family rooms, a pool, and tons of laundry every week. Clare enjoyed cleaning her house as it gave her time to think. Besides, she always enjoyed talking to Peter, Martha's father, who lived there for the winter. Poor guy was battling bladder cancer, but he always seemed to be in a peachy mood. He gave her great advice on what to do, but he was also a big flirt, so she would have to ignore him and head off into another room.

Clare glanced over at the clock on the wall; it read 7:00 a.m., which gave her plenty of time before they had to leave. She noticed Brenda wasn't home yet from her early morning job. She was cleaning the bar/restaurant every morning around 4:00 a.m. and it usually took her a couple of hours. Who knows, maybe it was in bad shape this morning and needed extra love.

Clare hated filling in for her because the bar stank and reminded her of Jim. The smell of booze made her want to gag. One time in the men's restroom, someone had the runs and it looked like they were trying to lift up the seat as they were crapping but it went everywhere. She had to cover her nose and mouth so she wouldn't breathe in the stench.

She finished packing her lunch for the day when Brenda came walking in the door.

"So, how was the bar this morning?"

"Not too bad today."

"What took you so long? Thought you would've been finished by now, it's after 7:00 a.m."

"I got some gas for my car and picked up donuts for us this morning."

"Oh, I don't eat this early, but thank you for thinking of us. Maybe Kayla will eat one." She cut up a donut and went into the living room where Kayla was watching the *Wiggles*.

"Here, sweetie, eat some breakfast." Kayla didn't move her eyes fixed on the TV. She popped a piece in her mouth and continued to watch the show.

Brenda and Clare headed out onto the lanai to have their morning talk and coffee.

"So, if you don't mind me asking, what was the call about last night?" Brenda asked.

"Guess who?" I thought I'd shut off the ringer before going to bed last night. Sorry I woke you up."

"What did he want at that time in the morning?"

"Drunk as usual. Oh, and he wanted to say goodbye because he was going to kill himself."

"Why does he say that to you? Do you believe he'd do it?"

"I don't know, but I hope not. I don't know how I'd live with myself if he did. How would I explain it to Kayla? 'Sorry, sweetheart, your dad killed himself because Mommy left him.' She'd never forgive me, but I also wouldn't tell her like that either. I don't want to even think about it."

"I wouldn't know what to say either, but you can't keep blaming yourself for what he does. That's all his business — you don't make him do the things he does."

"I know. I keep telling myself that over and over. One day it will sink in, I'm sure." She glanced at her cell phone. "Oh, crap! I have to leave. See you later, Brenda."

"I'm working tonight at Pizza Hut, so I will see you in the morning."

"Okay, have a good day." Clare raced inside, turned off the television, and carried Kayla to the door, putting her shoes as she went. She grabbed their bags and headed out of the door.

Nineteen

Detective Parks-Chicago

Setting the phone down in its cradle, Detective Parks reached for a cigarette. He'd just got off the phone with his father, who called to ask if he'd fly back down to Florida and check out the house. His parents lived in Illinois in the summer, so no one was down there to stay at the house in Naples. Apparently, there had been some break-ins around their area.

Searching for flights, he was able to find one that left the following morning at 9:30 a.m. After finishing his cigarette, he packed a small bag because he was only planning to stay for a couple of days. Besides, he always kept extra clothing down there in the guest room.

****

The next morning, as he sat waiting for his plane to arrive, he dug in his briefcase and pulled out a file that Detective Brown had given him. Brown had asked if he'd look over a case that was forwarded to him. Since he was going down to Naples, he suggested that he might help the local police solve the case they'd stumbled upon a few weeks ago. Most of the time, they didn't go outside their jurisdiction, but Detective Parks was a well-known detective who was good at his job. The file didn't seem to list much evidence. He read over the information they'd collated and scanned the photos of the body they'd found at a beach near his parents' house.

The victim had been stabbed multiple times in the chest and lower abdominal region. The police searched her condo, but found no one else's prints. In fact, it looked as if the place had been scrubbed clean, so the perpetrator knew what to use to get rid of the blood and evidence. Reports on the interviews with the other people in the condominium building stated they never saw her come in or out. Those who did see her said she was always alone.

Scrolling down, his eyes caught a phrase he had seen before in another case. It seemed that one of the witnesses remembered hearing and seeing a motorcycle. In fact, two interviews substantiated seeing a motorcycle. The clock on the wall showed 8:45 a.m., so he placed the file back in his briefcase and stood to stretch.

He opened his cell phone and called Detective Brown to ask if he could fax some papers to the house down in Florida. Parks told him that the file he'd given him seemed familiar and that it may match a couple of cases he'd worked on in Ohio in the past. *Hell, there could even be more bodies out there that they didn't know about,* he thought. He finished the conversation and boarded the plane.

Twenty

Jim

Jim chugged down two more beers after his conversation with Clare. Setting down the phone on the table in front of him, his thoughts began to unravel. He couldn't quite understand why she didn't want to be with him. He was a good-looking man and pretty good in bed. Chuckling aloud, he opened another beer and lit a cigarette.

He sat on the balcony and remembered the time he'd spent with her. He didn't see why she wasn't happy with him. She's the one with the problem. All she does is work all day, then comes home and does more work around the house. She doesn't even participate in bed anymore. It's like having sex with a dead person. All she does is crawl into bed and go to sleep. She doesn't even acknowledge that I am in bed with her. She claims she's always too tired. Too tired from what? Cleaning homes all day. Hell, I could that.

Besides, she needs to be cut down and told what's wrong with her — every woman does. It seems that everything goes to shit when you get married and have a kid. You stop spending time with each other because you're always too busy taking care of the kids. What about me? I need affection too; I need to have sex and feel like a man. If she isn't going to give it to me, then I will find it somewhere else. Some woman out there will have sex with me when I want it, even if it is every night.

Clare always said we didn't need sex all the time to fulfill our relationship, though it couldn't hurt if we did. Jim set his half-empty beer can down in front of him got up from the chair and then staggered into the house to make his way to the bathroom. He lifted the lid of the toilet and puked, then lay down on the floor next to the toilet.

He awoke hours later with his mouth tasting nasty like raw fish. Reaching for the bathtub, he pushed himself up. He stood in front of the mirror and rinsed out his mouth with water. Glancing in the mirror at his pale complexion, he shut off the water. He then walked into the kitchen and made a pot of coffee.

Scanning the room, he noticed Clare had taken all of her Elvis collectibles. He wondered why she'd done that. She probably thought I'd destroy them like I did before.

Oh well, she deserved it; I don't know why she collected that stuff anyway. Jim turned and peered at the clock on the wall. *Oh, wow! It's 11:00 a.m. already?*

He poured a cup of coffee and headed out onto the patio. He sat there smoking his cigarette, then reached for his phone and started to call Clare. All of a sudden, he got a sharp piercing pain in his gut; he bolted to the bathroom and vomited again. Making his way back to the sofa, he lay down and fell back to sleep.

More hours had passed when he awoke and noticed it was going on 4:00 p.m. He reached for the arm of the sofa and pushed himself up. He poured another cup of coffee and put it in the microwave to heat up, then strolled to the chair outside.

Picking up the phone, he dialed his mom's number and waited for her to answer. They talked for almost an hour about Clare leaving him. His mom didn't like him drinking and knew what he was like when he did. Clare had already warned him that she'd leave but, like always, he never thought she would.

He knew his mom was right; she always was when he asked her for advice, but did he ever listen? He never took anyone's advice, not even Clare's. He loved his mom very much, but he didn't know how to overcome his drinking problem. He just felt more confident when he drank, like he was *unstoppable*.

Before he ended the call, his mom told him to give Clare time to think. He told her he would, but he knew deep down he couldn't, because he thought she wouldn't come back to him if he did. She'd left him for good; he was certain.

He tried not to call her but his willpower wasn't strong enough. Before calling her, he thought it'd be a good idea to let work know he was sorry for not calling in that morning, that he was sick and had been in bed all day. He began to dial the number when it dawned on him that he'd never called any of his workplaces before, Clare always took care of that when he drank. He'd just stick to the story and not go into detail.

After talking to his boss, he hung up and called the friend he needed to help him get Clare back into his life.

"Hello," the voice said on the other end.

"Hey, Bob, it's me, Jim. Hope I didn't catch you at a bad time?"

"Of course you didn't. Just surprised to hear from you, is all."

Jim had met Bob a year ago at Daniel Penning, the rehab facility, when he was brought in for having the .357 magnum and saying he was going to kill himself. Bob had been brought in for drug and alcohol abuse. It was either jail or rehab and Bob said there was no way he was going back to jail.

Since then they'd hit several meetings together, but Jim went out boozing it up again, so Bob kept his distance from Jim and let him screw up his life.

"Well, I…" Jim paused, not knowing how to say what was on his mind.

"Well what? Why are you calling me?"

"I need…" Jim brushed the sweat from his forehead.

"You need what, Jim?"

"I need help, Bob! I need to get sober. Clare left me and took Kayla with her."

"I'm sorry, man, I really am, but I can't say I didn't warn you she'd leave one day."

"Yeah, I know, but I just can't do this on my own. Apparently, I called my boss last night and told him I wouldn't be coming in to work because I was going to commit suicide. I don't remember calling him or even saying that. I don't know what to do now. I've lost my family and now my job. I can't go on like this anymore, Bob. I need your help. Please, please help me." Jim fumbled for a cigarette and lit one up.

"Jim, if you are serious this time, then yes, I will help you, but under no circumstances can you hide anything from me. I will meet you at the Double A Club tonight at 7:00 p.m. Be early, I have some friends I want you to meet."

"Thanks, Bob, for everything. I'll be there."

"Good, I hope you will or don't bother calling me again."

"I will be there. That's a promise."

"No need for promises. If you truly want to get help then you'll show up," Bob said to him before hanging up the phone.

Jim sat thinking of the last time he tried to get sober. He went to meetings several times a week and things were going good until he met Pam. Pam was in the program and went to the same meetings he did. She was the woman he was going to divorce Clare for a couple of months ago. They got along great and hung out many times together. Of course, he had to tell Clare something else. He couldn't tell her he was seeing someone. He made Clare think he was hanging out with some of the people from the program, but as time went by Clare found out.

He claimed that Pam wouldn't sleep with him because he was married, which was a big lie as they had slept together many times. He also knew that Clare had talked to an attorney because he looked at her scheduling book when she was in the shower one night. The funny thing was, he never actually wanted the divorce. He guessed he just wanted his cake and eat it too. Clare was good to him, so why would he want to throw all that away? But he also had feelings for Pam.

The next day, Pam called and told him she didn't want anything more to do with him.

That's when he told Clare he didn't want the divorce; inside he knew he couldn't live without her. He knew she didn't trust him and he had to prove to her that she could. He didn't know how Clare found out he was drinking again. He'd spent his weekend with his so-called friend Dan. They went out for something to eat and ordered a couple of beers. All he knew was, when she came home that Sunday afternoon, she said she was moving out in a few weeks.

Apparently, he'd called her friend Brenda and asked her to come over, saying that he wanted to talk to her.

He couldn't really remember even asking if she wanted to watch a porno movie with him. Next thing he knew, Clare said she was leaving him. Jim tried to deny everything, but she called him some names and a liar; she didn't believe anything he told her. She was sick and tired of living a life of abuse and lies. Their relationship was finally over. Last night he came home to a half-empty condo. She'd finally kept her word.

He didn't know where she was staying or who with, but he could guess her leaving had something to do with Brenda. Ever since she came down to Florida, hell, ever since she met her in Ohio, she'd been trying to get them apart. Now he could say she'd succeeded.

Jim had been trying to tell Clare that Brenda was not a friend and that she would stab Clare in the back. He really didn't like that girl. Jim did call her that night and asked her to come over, but he was excessively drunk to remember anything after that. They just didn't get along. Jim had no doubt that she had called Clare and told her everything. That's okay; payback was a bitch. She'd get what was coming to her. That girl was just bad news and Clare was too blind to see it. Jim didn't know why Brenda even came down to Florida. She told them it was because she wanted to be near Clare. But leaving her job and moving to a new place without consulting her ex-husband about taking their daughter out of state was a dumb move. She found out the hard way when she went to court and lost custody of their daughter. He just didn't want to see Clare be taken for a ride. Brenda would use her, but Clare didn't believe a word he told her, so he decided to step back and let her see for herself.

****

Jim made one more call before putting out his cigarette and then headed inside to get ready for the meeting tonight. After he showered and got dressed, he opened the refrigerator to get something to eat. He made a sandwich and had another cup of coffee before going out.

He pulled into the parking lot near where the meeting was being held. Parking the truck, he hesitated before getting out. His stomach clenched and sweat beaded on his face.

He wasn't sure he could do this again, or if he was even ready to quit, but he knew he had to if, he wanted his family back.

Bob met him at the door and introduced him to many new people who were more than willing to take him under their wing. He knew it was now or never. He walked into the meeting room and sat down.

After the meeting, groups of people started to mingle, but Jim sat for a while longer before meeting with Bob and his friends.

Jim overheard them talking about a body that was found on the beach a couple of weeks ago.

"Apparently, the body was dumped in a hole in the sand and covered up, but the water eventually made its way up the shore and washed the sand away," said one of the ladies who was standing next to Bob.

"I heard about that," Bob replied. Jim's head came up as they continued to gossip about the body.

"The sad part was, I knew the girl who was killed. We used to go to school together," the same woman said. Jim felt dizzy and his body trembled as he waited for more information about the body. He needed to know if it was the same girl, he'd slept with.

"What was her name?" Jim asked, trying not to sound suspicious.

"Shannon Crumb." Hearing her name made his stomach flip. He swallowed hard, trying to keep down the food he'd eaten earlier.

"I met her about six or seven months ago at an art show on Fifth Avenue. Shannon talked about a guy she'd met at a bar, but never mentioned his name. The police are checking her place now," the woman added.

"Well, I hope they find whoever did this to her," Bob replied. "It makes me cringe to think there is someone out there on the loose, getting away with it."

Jim excused himself to use the restroom. After splashing water on his face, he looked into the mirror. Visions flashed through his head as he recalled being with her. As he splashed on more water, he shook his head trying to make all the images stop. Gaining control of himself, he hurried out of the restroom and chatted with Bob before leaving for home.

Home was where he needed to be; he had to relive what his mind was already telling him. Good or bad — he was going to figure it out.

Twenty-One

Present time…

"I wasn't quite sure if I needed to kill Jim. Just by watching him, I knew he'd kill himself by drinking in time. Although, I suppose a gun would be quicker, or a knife which *I* prefer to use. I should have ended his pain sooner and given my friend her life back. No one deserves to go through life being afraid of their own spouse and always wondering what they were going to do next. But I had to give her some credit: she'd finally made a step towards a new life. I just wish it hadn't been with Brenda."

"Why does it matter that Brenda helped her to leave?"

I laugh. "Brenda cannot be trusted. Sure, she tries to be a friend to Clare, but she has secrets of her own."

"Would you mind sharing them with me?"

"Well, for one, she uses people. Brenda thinks of only herself. I would say Jim and her make the perfect couple, but Jim can't stand the person Brenda is, which in turn is exactly the way *he* is. Although, what do they say? 'Outside the woods you can see everything, but when you're in the woods you are blind of the truth' or something like that. Second, Brenda is a lying bitch. She wants Clare to believe that she hates Jim and vice versa, but we'll get to that later.

"Then there's that Detective Parks nosing around. I saw him when I was in Ohio after the first two killings, but I covered my tracks well so he wasn't able to solve the case. I have a police scanner that I listen to and sometimes I like to hang around the station. You know, to see who's coming and going. That's when I saw him pull into the parking lot and get out of his car. He was talking to a Detective Malarkey. I wouldn't be surprised if they called him to solve the case. Doesn't matter really, I still have more of the story to tell.

Twenty-Two

Clare

Clare looked at her cell phone, it was almost 4:30 p.m. *Good, time to go*, she thought. Her mind wasn't on her work today as she folded up towels in the laundry room. All she had to do was put the clothes and towels away then she was done for the day.

She closed the trunk and slid behind the wheel. She took a moment and adjusted her seatbelt, then took her phone out of her back pocket and set it in the cup holder. She turned up the radio to relax; feeling the sound of the drums beating as she began tapping the steering wheel. The music was flowing through her body when her phone rang. Jim's name appeared. "Oh great, what now," she mumbled.

"Hello."

"Hey, Clare, what you're doing?"

"I'm driving. I see you didn't kill yourself after all," she replied, not trying to sound funny.

"I honestly don't remember saying that, Clare and I'm sorry that I did. I guess I had too much to drink last night."

"You could say so. Look, I don't want to fight with you. What do you want to talk about this time?"

"Clare, I lost my job today, I don't know how I am going to pay the bills. Will you please come back? I'm sorry for saying what I did and doing what I did. I love you and want you to come home. Please! I can't live without you."

"Technically, you can. You lived without me before I was ever in your life so you can live without me now. All you want is for me to come back and take care of everything again. I'm not going to do that, Jim. You need to quit drinking because it's not doing anything for you and it's making my life a living hell and those around you."

"I'm sorry for everything. I want you to know that I'm going to a meeting tonight with Bob. I'm not going to drink anymore."

"So, you're saying that you want me to come back after, what, twelve hours of not drinking?" Clare chuckled into the receiver. "Please, you think I'm that stupid? No, I'm not coming back, so just leave me alone. I need time to think and clear my head, and you need to get sober and find a job because I'm not going to pay your bills too."

"I don't know what your problem is, Clare," he huffed, "but I love you and I will fight for you. I will get you back and we will be a family again. Besides, Kayla needs me; she needs her father."

"A family? You don't know what a family is, Jim! All you care about is getting drunk. You told me when you started drinking that you had four years of making up to do. Well, I have seen enough and put up with too much, so don't expect me to come back just yet." *Why doesn't he get it? I don't want to live with his drinking anymore and now he is trying to use Kayla against me. Saying that we should stay together because of her. Does he think I'm going to sit back and let her grow up in such an environment? Watching her dad get drunk, throwing things, and cutting me down? No way am I going to put her through that. My mind is already screwed up; I don't want hers to be too,* she thought.

"Clare, are you there?"

"Yeah, I'm here. Just thinking as always."

"I didn't call to fight, I just wanted you to know that I made a decision to get help and make myself better. I wanted you to be the first to know."

"Thanks for thinking of me. I hope you stay sober and make it work."

"I will, but only because I want you back. I've got to get ready now, so I'll talk with you later."

"Sure, talk later." Clare shut her phone. She picked up Kayla and headed to their new home. They ate dinner, watched some TV and then she gave Kayla a bath and put her to bed.

Clare sat on the lanai watching the palm trees blow in the wind. The sound of her phone ringing brought her back to reality. She saw it was Dan.

"Hey, you, what's going on?" she said when she answered the phone.

Dan gave out a deep laugh. "Is that how you answer the phone these days?"

"Only when I see that it's you calling. So, how's it going?"

"I'm good. Just thought I would give you a buzz. I heard you've left Jim."

"Wow! Word travels fast. Let me guess, Jim called you last night too?"

"Yeah, but actually he came to my place about 1:00 a.m. drunk off his ass. Asked if you were in my condo. I asked him why would you be at my place. That's when he said you'd packed your things and left before he came home from work."

"Does it surprise you that I left?"

"No, why should it? I knew what he was doing behind your back and you needed to know. I think it's about time

224

you left him. Especially after that day when you came over to my place and said we couldn't be friends anymore after he'd tossed you around and slapped you and then broke your cell phone in half."

"Oh, yeah, I remember that day." Jim had been on one of his rampages. He accused her of sleeping with Dan once again, took her client book, and started ripping pages out of it. She tried to fight him, but he was much stronger than her. He took her phone and snapped it in half. When the fight was over, her body was sore like she'd been hit by a freight train.

"So, where are you staying? And don't worry, I won't tell Jim where you are."

"Well, I guess I can trust you, since you've been honest with me about his drinking. Besides if you tell him and he shows up here, I'll come over and kick your ass."

Dan laughed into the phone. "I'm scared now."

Laughing with him, Clare said. "You should be. I'm staying with Brenda in Clayview Estates. Right down the road from you."

"I know where that's located. Good for you, Clare. You deserve a better life."

"That's what people tell me, so I guess they're right."

"Would you like to get together sometime and watch a movie or go for a ride on my bike?"

Did she just hear him right? Did he just ask her out? But I'm still married to Jim so it wouldn't be right, but we are friends and it doesn't mean we have to sleep together. I guess it wouldn't hurt to hang out with him, she mused. "That sounds like fun. Maybe we could get together."

"How about this Friday? Do you have any plans?"

"Friday sounds good, but I'll have to check with Brenda and make sure she can watch Kayla for me."

"Good, I'll speak with you by Friday then. Clare, you don't have to worry about me. We're friends, right?"

She couldn't believe he had just read her mind. "Yes, we are friends. Talk to you soon, Dan." She stared at her phone as she closed it; still trying to decide if going out with Dan was a good idea. They always had a great time together when he came over for dinner. She was attracted to him, she knew that, but she was scared: scared that he would one day hurt her. She didn't think she could handle another heartache from a man. She decided to call it a night, but this time she made sure her phone was turned off before climbing into bed.

****

The next few days flew by without any calls from her husband. She had lunch with Brenda on Friday and asked if she was free to watch Kayla. She said she could and the conversation turned to Dan.

226

That night, Clare was a nervous wreck. She took two showers and spent an hour trying to do her hair, which she ended up putting in a ponytail.

"You look great, Clare," was all Brenda said as she watched Clare.

"Why am I so nervous? We're just friends, that's all. I shouldn't go. I should just call him and tell him I couldn't find a sitter." Her heart pounded.

"Clare, stop it. You'll have fun. Just be you. You need this."

"Are you sure it's the right thing? I only left Jim a week ago."

"Yeah, you did, but Dan likes you and you'll have a good time."

"I guess you're right." Before she knew it, Dan was knocking on the door.

Brenda went to answer it.

"Hey, how are you doing, Brenda?"

"I'm good and you?"

"Same old, same old. Working a lot of hours. Is Clare ready?"

"Yeah, I'll get her." Brenda strolled into the bedroom where Clare was playing with Kayla. A few minutes later Clare appeared. She picked up her leather jacket and they stepped outside.

"You look great, Clare," Dan murmured as he stared at her.

"Thanks. I wasn't sure what to wear, so I hope this will be okay." She smiled up at him. She had decided on jeans and a nice dress shirt.

"Like I said, you look good." They walked down the stairs and over to his motorcycle. She waited until he started the bike and then hopped on. The wind ruffled her hair as they glided down the road. They rode into Bonita Springs and had dinner. They talked and laughed about everything. She felt comfortable around him and was glad she could be herself. After dinner, they rode to the beach and sat on the sand, listening to the waves hitting the shore. The sky was filled with stars that shone brightly above them. There wasn't a single cloud in the sky that night. Clare felt as though she was dreaming this night with him. Dan was a gentleman and he didn't make her feel afraid or nervous. After driving back to Brenda's place, he pulled into the parking lot and shut off the bike. They stood outside and talked for what seemed like hours.

On Saturday, Brenda, Kayla, and Clare spent their time at the beach soaking up the sun and swimming. Clare tried to keep her mind off Dan, but he seemed to be all she could think about. She wondered if he was replaying the night they shared together.

On the way home from the beach, they stopped in to see Grammy. Sometimes it was hard for Grammy to get away from work so Clare took Kayla to her place of employment. Clare didn't talk to Grammy about Jim, it was one thing she had to learn not to do. There were days that continued to haunt her. Memories crept up on her when she least expected. She felt like moving away somewhere, but knew she couldn't escape from herself.

A few weeks after staying with Brenda, they found out she couldn't live there with Kayla anymore. Apparently, when Brenda got the condo, through some guy she worked with, she never signed a lease and that meant she shouldn't be living there. But after paying a small fine, Brenda had talked them into letting her stay. However, Clare had to go because the documents stated that there were to be no sub-tenants, so now Clare had to figure out where to live. She didn't have enough money set aside for her own place yet. She looked in the newspaper for something reasonable, but nothing was available to fit her needs. She would have to move back in with Jim.

Packing their things, she loaded up the car and said goodbye to Brenda. She pulled into the parking lot and stopped the car. Loading her arms with some of her belongings, she made her way upstairs to the condo. When she entered the house, she knew that Jim wasn't home. She'd texted him earlier and told him about the situation and that she needed to stay for a while until she found her own place. He, of course, said, "No problem," and told her that he wouldn't be there until later that night. The place was clean and smelled good, like he'd scoured it before she came. The night before she'd called and talked to Dan filling him in on what had happened.

That evening, she explained to Jim that she was going to be sleeping in the same room as Kayla and not their old room. She laid a mattress down on the floor across from their daughter's bed. After a couple of nights of sleeping in Kayla's room, she felt like she was being watched. One night, she opened her eyes and saw Jim leaning against the wall watching her sleep. Startled, she sat up in bed and asked, "What are you doing?" With no reply, he left the room and she lay back down. Staring at the ceiling, she couldn't shake the feeling of his eyes on her. The next morning she couldn't bring herself to ask him what he was doing in there last night. She went through her morning routine like any other day.

****

The summer season had begun before Clare was able to get a place of her own. She found a place in Countrytown, a gated community, mostly for older folks who were seasonal and who liked playing golf. The place had a pool nearby for all the residents who lived there, which would be nice in the summer because most of the residents went back up north.

The condominiums where painted an awful light blue with a pink trim, but for the price and location she didn't care what it looked like. It was now their home.

Jim was kind enough to help them move into their own place. Within two days, Clare had everything unpacked and pictures hung on the wall, but it took a couple of months before she felt comfortable sleeping without her daughter next to her. She always had a fear that Jim would come to the condo at night and do something to her. Although she lived in a gated community, she knew that wouldn't stop him from getting in.

Twenty-Three

Detective Parks-Florida

The few days Parks thought he'd spend in Florida turned into three weeks and then five. He worked day and night trying to fit the pieces of the case together, but he was getting nowhere. He sat down at the Victorian desk in his father's office, shuffling through the old case files for what felt like the tenth time. This time he decided to read every word written to make sure he wasn't missing something. He started with the section outlining what the witnesses saw and heard. He read over the conversations between the police and witnesses.

"I don't know what type of motorcycle it was, but it was pretty loud. Could be a Harley, I suppose, but I know they all sound the same these days. So, I can't say that it was or wasn't," the witness was quoted as saying.

"How many times has that motorcycle been here?" the officer asked.

"Maybe two or three times a week. No, make that two times a week."

"Did you happen to see who was driving the motorcycle?"

"I can't be sure."

"So, you don't know if it was a man or a woman?"

"I'm almost certain it was a man. That bike was too big for a woman to ride."

"I thought you said you didn't know what kind of motorcycle it was."

"Yes, that's right. But I've seen it from a distance and it looked pretty big."

Scrolling down, he read the statement from the second witness. The officer asked the same questions and the answers were the same except for one. After checking the other case from Ohio, he saw the only difference was that a lady walking her dog saw the motorcycle drive in and when the person got off she could see the shadow of the visitor. She couldn't determine the actual size of the person, but she was certain it was a man averaging five foot five to five foot eleven, but it was too dark to see his features to be sure.

He studied each case, dissecting it and jotting down his questions on a separate paper. He reached for the phone on the desk and dialed a number.

He knew Detective Malarkey very well. They had worked together on many cases in Chicago before Malarkey moved down to Naples to get away from the rampant crime. Whenever Detective Parks had a chance to come down to Florida, he made it a point to catch up with him.

"I'll see you in an hour then." Hanging up the phone, he gathered the files and his notes, then strolled downstairs.

Before leaving, he sat outside and tried to put more of the pieces together. He had read and reread the files. Coincidence or not, there were too many similarities to the killings in Ohio. After talking with Detective Malarkey, he would have a better idea of the details on the case. Although much of the evidence didn't add up, he would do what he could and not give up. He would discover who had committed the crimes and put the perpetrator away for a long time.

He pulled into Mel's Diner on Tamiami Trail and entered the restaurant. When he didn't see his old partner, he took an isolated booth in the far corner. He sat with his back against the wall to face the entrance. Flipping through the files, he looked up just as the detective walked through the door and he waved him over.

"Hey, old pal. How's it been going for you up in the cold snow? Getting tired of it yet? I can always get you a job down here. We could use someone like you," Detective Malarkey greeted him.

"I'm doing well, staying busy as usual. You know how it is up there. Every week there's a missing person or dead body floating around. It's Chicago, what do you expect?" Detective Parks replied while taking a sip of his coffee. "Besides, I like it up there in the country, Naples is too much like a city for me to move here."

"Suit yourself, but I'm glad you came when you did because it seems like we have another body on our hands as of yesterday."

"Did you bring the case file with you?"

"I'd thought you'd ask." Detective Malarkey pulled the case file out of his leather pouch and slid it across the table.

"Her name is Pam Grayer. Pretty thing she was. Her mother and father live in South Dakota. We phoned them and they are on their way. It's a real tragedy, these women. Whoever is doing this has a lot of anger."

"Why do you say that?"

"Take a look at the photos and you'll see. There's no remorse. This person kept stabbing them, even after they were dead. You can tell by the stab wounds that the perpetrator didn't hesitate: he just continued slashing." Detective Malarkey waved his hand at the waitress walking by and ordered an unsweetened iced tea with no lemon.

Parks studied each photo, scanning every detail. "I can tell you what they were using as a knife, but I would like to see the other body before I finalize my theory." He paused and closed the file when the waitress brought the glass to the table.

"Sure, we can do that when we're done here." Detective Malarkey grabbed two Splendas and tore the packets open, then stirred them into his iced tea.

Detective Parks read the witness statements. Once again, he saw that there was a motorcycle appearing at the scene before each murder. He couldn't say for sure if that was the killer, but it was just too coincidental not to be. They sat discussing the cases before heading off to see the coroner. He'd take a closer look at all the files later once he got back to the house. He wanted to cross-check them with the cases from Ohio to see if he could find more similarities between the victims.

****

Detective Parks stretched his arms above his head. He'd been studying the four cases for hours since he arrived back at the house. He'd inspected the bodies with the coroner and asked for the results of hair, skin tissue and anything that had been found before he got there. The coroner said the results would be faxed over as soon as he had them. He jotted down a note to make a trip to each of the victims' homes and investigate the crime scenes for himself.

It was nearly 1:00 a.m. when he finally decided to take a break and get some sleep. He needed to give the information time to sink in; he'd take a fresh look at it in the morning.

Twenty-Four

Clare

Clare organized her desk in the den. She had been getting back into writing her novel that she started when she left Ohio. So much had been going on this past year that she didn't even think about it, but she had more time in the evening now she wasn't living with Jim. She was able to relax and spend time getting to know herself again. Sure, it was a little lonely, but Kayla kept her busy during the day and she wrote at night.

When she'd finished, she grabbed her purse and sweater from the chair and walked into Kayla's room.

"Time to go, sweetie."

"I can't wait to see Carrie! I've been wanting to go to her house so really bad," Kayla replied.

"So really bad, huh?" Clare smiled at her daughter. "You're too cute, sweetie."

"Momma, I love you so, so, so, so, so much in the whole, whole wide world." Kayla wrapped her arms around Clare's legs.

"You do, do you? Well, I love you so much, more than the whole world and the universe put together." Clare rubbed Kayla's back.

"I love you more."

"And I love you most." Squatting down, she gave Kayla a kiss and hug before they went through the door.

Following the directions, it only took ten minutes to get to Jillian's house. Clare had met her at the school one evening when she was picking up Kayla. Jillian introduced herself; she said they knew of Kayla from when she lived behind the school and when Jim took her to the pool on weekends. They continued talking as they walked to their cars and exchanged phone numbers so they could get together for a play date.

****

She pulled into the driveway behind a dark blue Impala. After Clare put the car in park, Kayla jumped out as her friend Carrie came running towards her. She smiled as she watched the excitement on her daughter's face. The girls took each other's hand and ran inside the house. Clare collected her purse on the front seat and climbed out of the car.

The house was a ranch-style home painted a crème white with beige shutters around the windows. A cement path made of small, multi-colored pebbles led to a basketball hoop near the line of sand and palm trees. She went to the front door that was left open by the girls and knocked as she stepped inside.

Clare called out, "Hello." A long hallway in front of her had three separate doors off to the right. Pictures of the kids hung on the walls, along with portraits of Jillian and her husband. To the left and center of the room was the family room.

A voice from another room replied. "Come on in." Jillian poked her head out from the kitchen, which was on the other side of the family room wall. Clare strolled inside, closing the door behind her.

"Hey, how are you doing?" Jillian asked with a sparkle in her eye and a bright smile.

"I'm doing well and you?"

"Busy as always. I just wanted to clean the kitchen before we sit down."

"That's fine. Do you need help?"

"What? No, you are my guest. Please sit down and relax. Would you care for anything to drink?"

"Sure, what do you have?"

"Coke, Sprite, water, or juice."

"I'll take a Sprite please." Jillian handed her a can. "Thank you." Clare set the can on the dining room table and it hissed as she opened it.

"Tom, my husband, would like to have Kayla and you stay for dinner tonight, if that's all right?" Jillian rinsed the washcloth out and hung it in the middle of the sink.

"That sounds nice. Thank you for asking." Lifting the can of Sprite, Clare took a sip.

She chatted with Jillian, who had joined her at the table. Minutes later, Jillian's husband waltzed in the room. His hair was a sandy blonde complemented by his deep blue eyes that reminded Clare of Dan.

Tom was wearing Levi jeans and a red button-down Polo shirt. He asked, "So, what are you ladies going to do today?" He opened the refrigerator and took out a can of Coke.

"First, Tom, let me introduce you. This is Clare Culback. We met at the school when we were picking up Carrie and Kayla. They used to live near us when we were in the condominium behind the school. Although Clare and I just met last week. Clare, this is my husband Tom."

"Nice to meet you. Jim told me all about you when I lived there," Clare said.

"I've heard a lot about you myself, but it's funny that Jim only referred to you as his wife and no name though, I have a feeling that what he told me isn't half true."

"What do you mean by that?" Clare asked, wishing she'd kept her mouth shut. She knew that Jim downgraded her. She'd heard it from other people, so it shouldn't surprise her that Tom O'Brien would comment on it.

"I'm sure he has said a lot about me to many people. Let me take some guesses." Clare listed several negative traits that Jim could have attributed to her.

"I didn't think it was true, what he said about you. Has he stopped drinking?" Tom asked.

"How did you know that he drinks?" Clare felt her face getting hot.

"He asked me questions when we met over at the condo. Said he was having a rough time quitting and that you were going to leave him if he didn't get help."

"Well, I can see it didn't matter if I left or not: he's still drinking."

"Tom here is six years sober. I thought many times of leaving him and taking the kids, but he fought it, and now we are so much happier and more of a family than all those years ago," Jillian said. "I would like to say stick it out, but I'm not in your shoes. You have to do what's best for you and Kayla, not what's best for Jim." Jillian reached across the table and squeezed Clare's hand.

"I can't live like that anymore, with his many suicide attempts and spending all our money on booze. Hell, I even lost count of the women he's slept with. Enough was enough and I just had to leave. God opened the door and I ran, not looking back." Clare looked up and studied Jillian's reaction and then Tom's. Their mouths were hanging open.

"If you ever need anything, please don't hesitate to ask us," Tom said.

"If you ever need to talk, we are here for you," Jillian added.

"Thanks, I could use a friend to talk to now and then," Clare said, then reached for her Sprite and took a couple of sips before setting it back down. "Enough about my life. What's for dinner tonight?"

"Chicken or steak on the grill okay with you?" Tom asked.

"Those are my favorites. I'd never pass up a steak on the grill," Clare replied, feeling more at ease. Talking about Jim always brought out an angry side of her she didn't much like, but it was what she had become these past couple of years. Maybe in time she wouldn't feel so angry and afraid of him, though she knew deep in her heart she still had feelings for him. She still held onto the old Jim she once loved and adored, but that Jim was gone.

Tom excused himself, saying he had some errands to run and a meeting to catch before dinner. Jillian and Clare strolled outside and sat by the pool where they talked about their kids and jobs. Jillian said she used to work at a bank and decided to become an accountant. She told Clare what it was like with Tom when he used to drink and life up in Connecticut before moving down here. Clare then spoke of her past and what it was like living in Ohio.

"I'm excited to start a new cleaning job this week. The house is huge; it's down by Port Royal, I think. I usually map it out before I go, so I'm not late getting there," Clare said.

"That's smart. I bet it's beautiful inside."

"I'll have to let you know after I go on Tuesday. The woman who owns the house phoned me from Illinois, saying that I was recommended to her from the cleaning girl she has now. I guess she moved back to her home town in New Jersey."

"Good for you, Clare, getting recommended by other people. I can't wait to hear all about it. Do you have any other homes that size?"

"No, that's the first one. They're willing to pay me seven hundred a month to clean their place every week. I can actually get rid of a cleaning or two. It will probably take me all day to do it. I'll have to rearrange my schedule with the people I work for now, or maybe I can fit everyone in and won't have to let anyone go."

"Your job sounds hectic."

"Not really, I love my work. I'm able to meet new people and see all kinds of homes."

They talked for hours about everything and anything. Tom came home and was outside cooking on the grill. The smell of the steaks made Clare's mouth water. Clare helped Jillian in the kitchen to get the food prepared, and then they sat outside by the pool eating dinner. The kids sat inside at the kitchen table laughing and having a good time. Dusk fell and crickets chirped in the grass. Enjoying her visit, Clare breathed in the night air.

****

Once they'd left and arrived home, Clare got Kayla ready for bed and tucked her in, kissing her on the forehead. "Sweet dreams, sweetie. I'll see you in the morning."

"Good night, Mommy. I love you."

"I love you too, sweetheart." Clare closed the door behind her and retreated to the kitchen. Pouring a glass of iced tea, she sat down to relax. She didn't feel much like writing tonight. Talking about Jim earlier had put her in a sour mood.

She flipped through the TV channels, but nothing appealed to her so she shut it off and walked out onto the balcony.

She dialed her friend Angel's number but there was no answer, so she left a message.

Twenty-Five

Detective Parks

Detective Parks pulled his car to a stop and killed the engine. He grabbed the files on the front seat and opened the door. He'd read the files of the two cases over and over and could tell you what had happened at each scene, but he also knew that people missed things, so he needed to sweep over the crime scene. There would always be something left behind.

From the trunk of his rental car, he took out the bag of crime scene equipment he'd borrowed from Detective Malarkey and strolled up the brick walk to the entrance, his hazel eyes scanning the parking lot and building. Instead of taking the elevator to the fourth floor, he climbed the stairs to the left. It was possible that the murderer could have taken the stairs and dropped something; anything and he'd be the one to find it.

Slipping on rubber gloves that he'd put in his jacket pocket, he entered the home of the victim, Shannon Crumb, who was found at the beach.

Inside, to his right on the wall, he found the light switch and turned it on. The kitchen was a contemporary style, with antique wooden boxes surrounding the tops of the cabinets.

He opened each cabinet inspecting the contents. This was his method of getting to know her, to walk in her steps. He didn't notice any of the knives missing because he'd checked and counted each one in its place. He was looking for a particular knife that was serrated on one side. Walking into the living room, he shuffled through the magazines on the coffee table and then a photo fell out onto the floor. He bent over and took it between his fingers. The photo was of Shannon, but whoever was in the photo with her had been removed. His finger followed the edges of the torn photo, thinking it was a good idea to hold on to it, he shoved it into the file. He reminded himself to check all the garbage cans for the other half. As he moved from the kitchen to the bedroom, his eyes went over the tiled floor for blood or anything else that would lead to the murderer. Nothing jumped out at him. Nothing told him that she was murdered here. He knelt down beside the bed and lifted the bed skirt to get a peek underneath. There were no dust bunnies, clothes, or even hair for that matter, under the bed — someone had cleaned this place.

Peeling back the comforter, he looked at the sheets. There wasn't one crease in them, they were clean and unwrinkled, like they were just put on the bed. He moved over to the nightstand on the other side of the bed and began opening every drawer. There were several other photos that he picked up and shuffled through, he then came across another ripped picture of the victim. He tossed all the photos into the file and finished checking the rest of the drawers before making his way into the bathroom.

He found nothing but the photos, but maybe that's all he needed. They were at least something. Before leaving, he walked around taking swab samples from the floor in all the rooms, even though there were no signs of blood.

Locking the door behind him, he took the elevator down to the entrance of the building. On the wall of the elevator was a smear mark. He opened his case, swabbed it, and used a solution to confirm what he already knew was blood. Taking another sample, he'd cross-check it with the body to determine if it belonged to Shannon Crumb.

Standing outside, he remembered what the witnesses had said in their report. He studied the location of the parking lot where the motorcycle was said to be parked. He noticed there were no streetlights in that part of the parking lot. No matter where you stood, no one could see anything at night, but he'd have to come back tonight and double-check his theory.

Tossing the files onto the front passenger seat, he dropped down behind the wheel. Taking the second victim's file, he opened it, read the address, and then started the car.

Arriving fifteen minutes later, he stood in the parking lot and scanned it he did the last one. Again, there was no lighting near where the motorcycle had been parked; it seemed this person didn't want to be seen on the nights they showed up.

This time he rode the elevator to the second floor. Inserting the key into the lock, he turned it but realized that it didn't click.

Hesitating, he turned the knob and opened the door. Once inside he glanced around and saw near his right foot was a vacuum and bucket.

"Hello, is anyone here?" he called out. Hearing a noise coming from the bedroom, he went to investigate. Stepping inside, he saw a light on in the bathroom.

"Hello, who's there?" He called louder this time. A sound came from the room like a can hitting the floor and then a woman walked out.

"Oh, sorry. I didn't know you'd be coming home this soon otherwise I would have come earlier," she said.

"Who are you?" Detective Parks snarled, resting his hand on his gun.

Clare stepped back. "I'm sorry. What?" She wiped her hands with the rag she was holding.

"What are you doing here and who are you?" His eyes searched every inch of her. She was beautiful, with her brown hair pulled into a ponytail and those green eyes. He was overcome by her beauty and forgot where he was.

"I'm Clare Culback, the cleaning girl you hired a few days ago."

"I don't live here."

"Then who are you?" she asked, feeling embarrassed and yet frightened at the same time.

"I'm Detective Terry Parks and I'm investigating the murder that took place here." He shifted from one foot to the other like a schoolboy talking to a girl for the first time. He asked, "Who called you to clean this place?"

"He said his name was Sam Elliot and that there would be a key under the front doormat and money on the counter. He gave me the address and day he wanted me to clean. I didn't know that this was a crime scene, honestly."

"How much have you cleaned?"

"I just got here ten minutes ago. I always start in the bathroom and then move on to the kitchen, so I haven't done much here. I'll get my supplies and be out of your way."

He couldn't believe how sexy she looked in her tan khaki shorts and white tank top. She was thin, but had a nice curve to her waist and short legs. Moving past him, she set her things by the bucket and vacuum she'd brought up with her.

Detective Parks stood behind her. "Is there anything else you can tell me about this Sam Elliot?"

"No, not really. Like I said, he called me and told me what he wanted done. Oh, wait, there is one thing. He asked if I'd use this cleaning product on the floors." She pointed to a bottle sitting on the counter near the cash he'd left her.

He walked over and picked up the bottle. "Don't you want your money?"

"No, you keep it and check for prints and whatever else you do."

"I take it you watch a lot of crime scene shows?" He let out a deep laugh.

Smiling back at him, she answered, "I watch my share of CSI and Bones." She bent over and lifted up her bucket, set it under her arm and placed her other carrying case filled with cleaning products in her hand. Then she opened the door and picked up her vacuum. "Nice to meet you. See you around some time." She closed the door behind her.

Detective Parks stared at the door. He heard her say something, but he was focusing on the bottle he was holding in his hands.

SERVPRO, in big letters across the front. He scanned the rest of the wording:

The best cleaning product you can buy for your worst spills. To remove and dispose of bodily fluids, tissue, and other potentially pathogenic substances resulting from accident, trauma, crime or death.* In big letters below, the bottle read: *SERVPRO CAN CLEAN AND RESTORE YOUR PROPERTY AFTER A CRIME SCENE INVESTIGATION. Also used for spoiled foods, human and animal waste.

After he set the bottle down on the counter, more questions popped into his head. He remembered reading about the first victim's condominium and that it was too clean to find any evidence. No blood, or anything at all for that matter.

He ran to the slider, unlocked it and pulled it open. He was hoping to catch this Clare Culback before she left. As he surveyed the parking lot, he didn't see her anywhere, not that he knew what she drove, but he did remember the vehicles that were out there when he came and noticed the dark green Saturn was gone. Now he had more questions to ask her. He would find out if she was at the other condo and was the one who had cleaned that. *But* what if he didn't see her again? He had ways of finding her though and if that's what he had to do, then he would.

Stepping back inside, he closed the slider and continued his search for photos. New clues were appearing each day he went over the files, so he wasn't going to work on another case until he had this one solved.

Checking all the drawers, starting in the living room and then the bedroom, he acknowledged they were all empty, except for clothes. There were no photos, not even paperwork or bills. He couldn't find anything. It was like someone had come in and emptied everything before he could search it. Walking back into the kitchen, he opened the garbage can and again nothing. He heard something land on the floor when he opened the lid. Moving the can aside, he found a crumpled piece of paper. Bending over, he picked it up and opened it, but it wasn't a piece of paper, it was a photo ripped on the edges, like the one he found earlier that morning — except this one looked like the other half.

Taking his file, the money, and bottle of SERVPRO, he strode out of the door and locked it behind him.

Sitting in his vehicle, he flipped open the first victim's file and took out the photos he'd found. He placed them alongside each other, and they fit together like puzzle pieces. The man in the photo had his arm around the victim. They were smiling: they were happy. Detective Parks sat staring at the two people. It was apparent that whoever ripped up the photo didn't want anyone to see him and her together, but the real question was, how did it get into the second victim's home.

Twenty-Six

Clare

"Hey, Brenda. Haven't heard from you in a while. Do you have time to talk?" Clare asked.

"Hi, yeah, sorry, just been working late at Pizza Hut every night. I need the money. You know how it is. So, what's up?" Brenda replied, yawning into the phone.

"Not much, was wondering how you've been lately." Clare then launched into telling Brenda about Detective Terry Parks and what happened at the condo where she was working a few minutes ago.

"Someone was actually killed there?"

"That's what he said."

"Did you notice anything while you were there cleaning?"

"No, but…"

"But what? You can tell me."

"There was this cleaner that was left for me to use. At the time I didn't think anything of it, until now."

"What cleaner? Come on, Clare, spill it."

"Well…" She paused. "It was for cleaning up blood spills. I read the bottle before I used it in the bathroom."

"No way. Are you serious? This is getting more exciting by the minute."

"Exciting? You have to be kidding me. This is some scary stuff, Brenda, and I don't want to be involved in any of it." Clare pushed a button to open the driver's side window, letting the air cool her down.

"What was the detective like?"

"What? Of all that information, you only want to know what Detective Parks looked like."

"Well, no, but I am curious. Is he tall, short, and good-looking? You have to tell me. You did talk to him, didn't you?"

"Yes, I talked to him, but I didn't ask him questions about himself." She cranked the wheel into a spot and cut the engine to continue her conversation with Brenda.

"Sorry, just think it's cool, you meeting a detective and all, but you're right, the important part is who was murdered there and why they called you to clean it up."

The words sank into Clare like lead. She didn't think of that. This person could've called anyone, but he called her instead. "Do you think I know the person who called me to clean that condo?"

"It's possible, or maybe they know you won't ask any questions and you do a good job. A job they didn't want to do."

"Maybe, but it's just too much right now. I don't want to think about a murder and that I was cleaning up the evidence."

"You mean you didn't clean the condo?"

"Didn't you hear me when I told you what happened?"

"You woke me up remember, it was all kind of hazy."

"I only got as far as the bathroom when he showed up. He told me his name and what had happened there, so I grabbed my things and left. I wasn't going to be the one to cover up the evidence and I would have if he hadn't showed up when he did."

"Oh." Brenda fell silent.

"Is everything okay, Brenda? You're quiet all of a sudden."

"Yeah, I'm fine."

"Hate to cut you short, but I've just arrived at my next cleaning, so I have to get off here."

"Oh, okay, I'll talk to you later."

"Sounds good. Have a good day."

Closing her cell phone, Clare opened the car door and got out. She spent the rest of the day thinking about the conversation she'd had with Brenda. She was acting weird, but Clare couldn't work out why.

Before going home, after her last house, she figured she'd try to find the new house she was starting tomorrow. "Wow," was all she mumbled as she drove by. The house looked bigger than she had imagined.

****

That evening Clare took Kayla to the park.

"Push me, Mommy!" Kayla demanded.

"Use your manners, please," Clare reminded her daughter as she gave her several big pushes. Clare sat down on the swing next to her.

"Mommy, how do you go so high?"

Clare pushed off and showed her how she would straighten her legs as she went up and then bring them in when she came down to move faster. "When you go up, have your legs out like you're trying to touch the sky. Then tuck them under you when you come down. In, out, in, out."

"Touch the sky." Kayla giggled.

"You're doing it, sweetie. Good job!" She remembered all the times they'd spent together; this was what life was all about. They both sat on the swings, swinging until the sun went down and then headed back home.

After putting Kayla to bed, she sat on the deck and her thoughts drifted to Detective Terry Parks. She wondered what he was doing at this hour, whether he was pouring over the case or watching TV. What he had for dinner and if there was someone to come home to every night. The phone rang bringing Clare back to reality; she jumped up and raced to it before it rang once more.

"Hello?"

"Hey, Clare. It's me, Dan."

"Hey you, it's been a long time since we've talked. How have you been?" Clare sat back down on the outside sofa and put her feet up on the table. Dan had moved from his one bedroom apartment to a townhouse in Ft. Myers, which was much closer to his work.

"I've been good. Just been thinking about you and was wondering what you've been doing."

"I'm all settled into my own place now. Been busy working." She filled him in on Jim and what he had been doing.

"Did you watch the news at six?"

"No, why! What happened?"

"It was about the two murders down there in Naples by you." Dan went on, "Looks like they may have found some new evidence in the second murder."

"What kind of evidence?" Clare bolted upright; listening to every word Dan had to say.

"I was at that condo earlier today."

"What? Why were you there?"

She told him her side of the story and the conversation with the detective.

"That's some heavy shit, Clare. And you don't know who called and asked you to clean?"

"No, I get quite a few calls to clean homes. I don't question the person calling or ask if it's a crime scene. I just clean it because I need the money. You are acting just as weird as Brenda was when I told her about what happened. Do you guys know something that you're not telling me?"

"What? I was just commenting on your story. Why would I know anything about the murders?" Dan's voice was rising. "I don't know those women who were killed, but maybe you should question your soon-to-be ex-husband about it. Maybe he knows them. Have you asked him the same questions and interrogated him?"

"Why, do you know something? Come on, Dan, if you know something, please tell me." She stood up and started pacing. She could feel in her bones that Dan was holding something back, but no matter how hard she tried, he didn't let on.

"I don't know for sure, but remember Jim has been acting weird and he is known to sleep around on you. I'm just saying, you should at least ask him."

"You don't think he's capable of killing anyone, do you? Please don't tell me that. I know we fought and sometimes I got hurt, but he never made any threats to kill me." Her mind wandered back in time, thinking if he could be the one killing these women. He never showed her any kind of violence in that way. *He wasn't a killer, was he?*

"Clare, are you there? I don't mean to alarm you, but Shannon Crumb is one of the women killed. She's the same woman he was cheating on you with."

"What? I didn't know her name. He never told me her name. I can't believe he'd be capable of killing someone."

"Do me a favor. The next time you talk to him, ask him in person and not on the phone. That way you can see his face. I know you hate him being close, but you could go to his work and ask him there. With people around so he won't do anything physical to you."

"That's true. Sorry, Dan, I didn't mean to lay this all on you."

"You didn't, I was the one who brought it up. I'm going to hang up now. Do me a favor and call me when you've spoken to him. I'd like to know what he has to say."

"I will. Thanks for calling me tonight. It was good hearing your voice again." Hanging up the phone, Clare then uncannily received a text from her husband wanting to know if she could stop at his place of employment and see him. She started to text to ask him why, but erased it and wrote *'Sure, where do you work?'* He texted the address and she wrote it down. She'd stop over after her cleaning tomorrow.

An idea popped into her head, so she hurried over to the computer. She searched for the two murders and photos of the women appeared on the monitor. They both had long blonde hair and blue eyes. They could've been twins, but she knew they weren't. Studying the images, she realized how beautiful they were and could see why he was so attracted to them. Her stomach flipped as she read the details of the murders. Clare didn't want to believe that her husband could be capable of murdering someone.

Flashbacks came of all the times he was caring and loving to her; even when he was angry. Although, he didn't show signs that he'd hurt her or Kayla, he did strut around with a gun or knife when he was drunk saying he was going to kill himself but never did it.

She was jumping to conclusions, but there were indicators that pointed to him. After printing out the photos of the women, she turned off the computer. She wanted to show Jim the images and see how he reacted. Although she knew he'd lie, because he always lied to her, she hoped his facial expressions would give him away.

****

The following morning Clare got up early. She'd spent most the night tossing, turning, and thinking of the worst of Jim.

After taking Kayla to school, she headed over to the new house to clean. Pulling into the drive, she opened her trunk and took out what she needed for the day. Unlocking the front door, she remembered the woman telling her that there was an alarm she'd have to shut off and then reset when she left.

Once in, she set her things down and went over to the keypad on the wall in the kitchen. A green light was flashing, indicating that the alarm was already disarmed. Confused, she checked to see if anyone was there.

"Excuse me! What are you doing in my house?" a deep voice said from behind her. She knew she'd heard that voice before. Clare whipped around and couldn't believe her eyes. "It's you. You live here?" she said.

Detective Parks raked a hand through his hair. "Well, actually it's my parents' home, but I'm staying here for a while to work on the case. I was hoping to see you again, Clare. I tried to catch you at the condo but you had already left." He poured himself a cup of coffee and asked, "Would you like a cup while we chat?"

"Well, I do have work to do." Shifting her feet, she realized she was acting like a teenage girl.

"This won't take long. I just have some questions for you. Please sit with me for a while." He motioned to the table and chairs outside.

She poured a cup of coffee and joined him on the patio. "So, what do you want to ask me?"

Detective Parks went back inside and retrieved his case file. He opened the cover and Clare got a glimpse of the photo of one of the victims. She shrieked at the sight.

"Oh, sorry. I didn't mean for you to see that." Before he had a chance to flip the picture over, she grabbed his hand.

"Do you mind if I take a closer look?"

"Why would you want to?"

She didn't want to tell him about her husband. "Just curious."

He handed her the stack of photos and she examined them. It was the same woman she had the printed pictures of that were in her car to show Jim.

"What is it?" She had tears welling up in her eyes. "What's wrong, Clare? Tell me."

"It's just horrible what has happened to them. That's all." She took a deep breath and looked through the rest of the photos. "What is it you wanted to ask me?"

"I wanted to know if you had cleaned her condo as well as the one where I saw you." He took a sip from his cup and set it down.

"I don't think so, but I would have to check my scheduling book. Why? What do you know?"

"Do you have your schedule with you?"

"Yes, it's in my car. I never leave home without it. I'll go get it." Once outside, she took several deep breaths, she then grabbed her book and went back inside. "What day do you want to know about?"

He thumbed through the file and told her the date.

"That's a Saturday. According to my book I wasn't working that day." Thinking back, she remembered Jim not being home that night as she had written down, 'Girl's night with Brenda,' but Brenda had some emergency and had to leave. *So, where was Jim and why did Brenda have to leave so quickly? Could they be sleeping together and not telling me?* She wondered.

"What's wrong, Clare? It's like you've seen a ghost."

"What?" she asked, shaking her head.

"You look like you were deep in thought."

"Sorry, I was just thinking back to what I did that day, that's all. It's nothing. Is there anything else you'd like to ask? I need to start cleaning because I have to pick up my daughter from school this afternoon." She was hoping that he was finished asking questions. She didn't want to have to lie to him anymore, but it would be against the law to hide evidence. He could then say she was involved somehow. But she wasn't sure what she knew, or didn't know for that matter. She'd have to talk with Jim first before saying anything to this detective.

"No, I don't have any further questions for you right now, but is there a number where I can reach you if something should come up?"

"Yeah, sure." She wrote her phone number on the piece of paper he offered and slid it over to him as he handed her his card.

"Thanks, I appreciate you talking with me. I'll let you do your job now."

"It's no problem, really." Clare could feel him watching her as she went back inside. She grabbed her cleaning bucket and some rags, then headed upstairs.

There were four bedrooms in the house, so she started with the farthest one. No one had been in the bedroom, so she freshened up the bathroom and dusted the furniture. Entering the second bedroom, which she could tell was the one Detective Parks had been sleeping in. She remade the bed, dusted, and cleaned the bathroom. Next to his room was an office with a large ornate desk and to the right was a huge computer monitor sitting on a dark brown antique bookcase; it was about waist-high, and there was a printer and some photos. On the left stood another antique bookcase, which was shoulder-high, with knickknacks and more photos.

Organizing the desk, she stacked the papers and files and then started to dust. Taking a second glance, she saw a photo sticking out of a file. She didn't like being nosy, but when she saw that it was a photo of Jim, she couldn't help herself. The photo was in a plastic bag, so she pulled the bag out of the file to get a better look. He was with a woman: the same woman she saw in the murder case file downstairs. The photo had been ripped and put back together with tape. Her heart sped up and her hands trembled as she gripped the photo with both hands.

She opened one of the files and read the first page. The case was in Ohio, not far from where they had lived. Thumbing through the papers, she noticed certain words highlighted, 'Knife wounds made in the chest and abdominal area.' The next file was highlighted as well, 'Buried in the sand near a lake. Both women have blonde hair.' Before thinking, she grabbed the file and bolted down the stairs in search of Detective Parks. When she spotted him outside still sitting at the table, she stormed out. "Where did you get this photo?" she demanded, trying to keep her cool but feeling her face getting hot.

"What are you doing with that?" he barked back.

"I should ask you that question. How did you get it and where may I ask did you find it?"

Before he said anything else, he motioned for her to sit down. Doing as he asked, she stared at him, waiting for an answer.

"First, I want to ask you, do you know the people in this photo? Then I'll tell you where I found it."

She nodded.

"Okay. I found the half with the woman on it at her condominium and the other half showing the guy at the second murder victim's condo where I met you. It didn't make sense to me at first, but now I have an idea that whoever killed these women either intentionally put the photo in the second woman's condo or dropped it without knowing. I was studying it and will have prints run on it later today. So, now you tell me who he is, since we both know who she is."

She wanted to think before she spoke but it was too late for that now. She could still question Jim later about the photo, though she knew he'd probably lie anyway. The detective would be straightforward with her. "The man in the photo is my husband. I had a feeling he was cheating on me, but this confirms it. I don't know the woman, but last year he was acting weird, like he was sneaking around. A couple of times his phone would ring and I looked at the number when he was in the other room. I wrote it down but didn't have the nerve to call the person back. I guess I didn't want to know for sure that he was cheating on me, again. I did question him about it, but he told me it was his sponsor calling and checking up on him. At the time, I didn't know that sponsors don't call you. You call them, unless of course, they are telling you about an event coming up, but it's your job to contact them every day. That's all I can tell you."

"I'm really sorry, Clare. Why do you stay with him if he continues to cheat on you?"

"Oh, we're not together. I left him a few months ago and filed for divorce. My daughter and I live in our own place now. What should I do? Is he a suspect in the murders?"

"Whatever you do, don't say a word to him. It may scare him and he'll run. Let me do more digging around. Do you have that phone number so I can confirm whether it was the victim calling him?"

She opened her cell phone and read him the number, then added, "I don't believe he is capable of killing anyone." Deep down she wanted to believe that he wouldn't hurt someone else. "When do you think you'll know?"

"A couple of days maybe, but I can try to get it sooner."

"Sorry about getting so upset. I'd better get back to work." She stood up and made her way to the door, feeling his eyes on her again just like she did earlier.

****

A few hours later, Clare finished mopping the floors and did her walk-through. Detective Parks had slipped into his room upstairs to wash while she finished downstairs. She emptied the bucket in the laundry room sink and gathered up her supplies. Opening the door, she carried her equipment and put it into the trunk. She sat in her car and debated whether or not she should see Jim as planned. Turning the key, she started her car, but a knock on the window made her jump. She lowered the window to hear what Detective Parks had to say.

"So, you were just going to leave without saying goodbye?"

"Sorry, I have a lot on my mind."

"We don't know each other well, but would you consider having dinner with me while I'm in town?" He smiled.

She was surprised by his invitation. She just wasn't sure if it was a good idea, but before she could stop herself, she heard herself say, "Sure, that sounds great, but I will have to let you when. I need to find a sitter first."

"Okay, then. Well, if you can't get a sitter, I don't mind if you bring her with you. I'd love to meet the little girl behind this beautiful woman."

He sure had a way with words. "I'll keep that in mind. Call me when you'd like to go out."

"Okay, I will. See you around, Clare."

She shifted the car into drive and rolled out of the driveway, leaving him standing there. She watched him in the rearview mirror before turning onto the main road.

She wanted to call Brenda and tell her all about her day, but her mind slipped to Jim. She had to see his face.

Five minutes later, she was pulling into the back parking lot of the store where he worked. She rang the doorbell to the back entrance and seconds later Jim opened the door.

"Hey, you're here! I have to get back up front. Come in." He turned and raced back through another door that led to the store. She followed, noting the back door was in the storage room. The shelves contained boxes that had writing on them. *Probably merchandise for the store*, she thought. There were two customers near the front looking through T-shirts and hats. It was a store filled with "Life is Great" clothes and hats for children and adults. Next to the register stood a revolving rack full of different flip-flops and sandals. Jim stood behind the counter as Clare leaned against the back near the racks.

"So, how's it been going? You look amazing by the way. It's been a while, Clare. I miss you." The look on his face was sad like a puppy begging for food. She didn't want to hear what he had to say right now; not when she had so much going through her head. *I wish he wouldn't look at me like that. He always makes me feel sorry for him and I end up taking him back.* The thoughts raced through her mind.

"I'm doing well and so is Kayla. She has been making friends in school. You haven't been to see her in a while. May I ask why?" she asked, searching his face for a reaction.

"Just been busy. Don't have time right now."

"Is that what I'm supposed to tell her, that her father doesn't have time to visit and spend the day with her? You're not much of a father, you know." Looking at his face, she couldn't tell if he cared for what she'd said or not. If he did, he didn't show any signs of it. Before she could stop herself, the words were out of her mouth. "Did you kill those women, Jim? Did you sleep with them, stab them to death, and then hide their bodies? Did you, did you do it?"

His face went pale as he stood there listening to the words she threw at him. He was speechless. He licked his lips to moisten them. He glanced cautiously around making sure no one was in the store to hear what she'd said.

"Are you worried that someone will hear me? Don't worry, I waited for the people to leave before questioning you."

"Clare, I didn't kill those women, I swear. Yes, I had sex with them, but I didn't kill them. You have to believe me."

Her heart sank like a ship to hear him actually say he had sex with them. She felt like crying, but she didn't want him to see her shed a tear for him. She'd shed too many tears for him in the past, but she was stronger now, wasn't she?

"I want to believe you, but you make it so hard. You betrayed our marriage and me. What am I supposed to think, Jim? Don't ask me to forgive you." She took in a deep breath. She needed to get out of there. "Look, I've got to go."

"Wait, Clare. Don't go. We aren't finished talking yet. Please, you have to believe me."

"Don't!" She threw up her hand. "Please, just don't say another word. I can't be near you right now. I have to go." She turned to walk away, but he grabbed her arm and twirled her around then kissed her on the lips. Pulling away, she shoved him backwards.

"Don't do that. You don't have the right to kiss me anymore. Just leave me alone, Jim." She stepped backwards, but he grabbed her by the throat and pushed her up against the wall.

"Please stop!" She gasped for air and tried to breathe through her nose but it was useless. Trying to unlatch his hand from her throat, she took in a couple more short breaths, she felt him unclench his hand when he heard the door chime. He appeared as if nothing had happened. She made a quick exit out the back door.

Sliding behind the wheel, she glanced in the rearview mirror to look at her neck. Ugly red finger marks from his grip covered her skin; she would have to cover them before picking up Kayla from school. She had to get as far away from him as she could.

By the time she'd reached the drive leading into her condo, it was nearly past 4:00 p.m. so she had plenty of time, but right now she needed time to think and clear her head.

She entered her home and hurried to the bathroom. She didn't wear much makeup, but she always bought cover-up in case she had a breakout. After finishing in the bathroom, she made her way to the living room, but she was bawling her eyes out before she sat down on the sofa.

Ten minutes passed, then twenty, before she was able to stop crying. She then wiped her nose and face. "How could he do that to me? He actually admitted he had slept with them. Not knowing was livable, but knowing — knowing hurt too much." She talked to the empty room wanting, no, hoping that her life would be happier one day and she wouldn't sit crying over what he'd done to her and their family. "What does he mean he doesn't have time for his daughter? Doesn't he want to see her? Doesn't he love her and want to be a father to her? Doesn't he care how she feels about him not spending time with her?"

Glancing at the clock on the wall, she grabbed her purse and checked her neck one last time before getting Kayla. She didn't want everyone to see her neck or puffy eyes and then ask if she was okay. She knew she would cry again and that wouldn't be a good thing, especially in front of people she didn't know.

That night she tucked her daughter in bed. She read her a story, then knelt down beside her and kissed her on the cheek. Before she could stop the words from slipping past her lips, she asked, "Does it bother you not to spend time with your dad? That he doesn't come to see you?"

Warmth surrounded her heart, as her daughter responded. "No, I have you, Mommy, that's all that matters to me. I am Mommy's girl, right? You will never leave me, right?" Tears started to form in Clare's eyes.

"Nope! I will never leave you, sweetheart. You are my baby bird and I will always love you. And yes, you are Mommy's girl." They hugged and Clare kissed her daughter on the lips before saying goodnight and leaving the room.

She was exhausted from all the crying she'd done today, so she retreated to her bedroom and crawled under the covers. The last thing she remembered was that she'd forgot to ask the detective about the file from Ohio, but would she or could she go to dinner with him? What if he saw her neck? Then he'd ask questions and she didn't want him discovering the truth about her marriage to Jim. She tried to hide things from her daughter and now she had to worry about the detective finding out what went on behind closed doors.

Twenty-Seven

Present time…

I received a message from Clare. I could tell by the few words she'd left that she wasn't doing well. I could tell she needed me, but I just couldn't call her back. I couldn't let her know what I was doing for her.

After I erased her message, I sat down outside and took a deep breath. The air was warm, and I could smell the salt from the Gulf making its way in. The sky was a seductive blue with no clouds in sight. I always enjoyed watching the sun come up in the morning and sipping my coffee as I reminisced on the past.

I remembered back when she worked at the factory, how hard she worked and never missed a day, at least not until she met that loser of a husband. He started calling her home at all hours of the night; I could tell by the look on her face that he was drinking again. I knew she didn't really want to go home to him, not when he was drinking.

She never said anything to me, but I knew by the way she moved that he had hurt her.

She told me that she blamed herself for his drinking because of what happened with Brent at the factory, but she doesn't know that he was drinking way before that.

Thanks to an old friend of hers from high school, I knew what he was doing behind her back: he was going to the bar in Orwell after work. This girl from high school told me she didn't know he was married because he didn't wear a ring. I should have told Clare about Jim years ago, but I thought I could take care of the problem myself. She told me that if she knew Jim had been drinking then she would never have married him, not after the last guy she'd dated.

—Now Brian, he was screwed up in the head. Not only did Brian drink, but also, he'd get so drunk, that he'd cut himself up with whatever he could find around his apartment. One day, she had enough of his psycho thinking and walked away, and never looked back.

I wish she could do that with Jim, but I guess it's different when you are married and have a child. My friend needs to find someone who will make her happy and love her for who she is. I can feel something is wrong and that my friend needs me, but what could be going on that would make her so defensive? And that detective guy Parks running out after she left the condo. What was up with that? She should've finished cleaning up what I'd missed, and she would have if it weren't for that detective guy Parks showing up when he did. Damn him! He almost caught me in Ohio because he stuck his nose in where it didn't belong. I bet if he hadn't come to Florida, I would have gotten away with the murders.

Twenty-Eight

Clare

Clare made dinner for Kayla and turned on the television. She wanted to watch the news, but decided to put on a program on for Kayla instead. After fixing herself something light to eat, she called Brenda to ask if she could watch Kayla on Friday.

"What's happening on Friday?" Brenda asked.

"Remember that detective I told you about? He wants to take me out to dinner. And knowing Jim, he wouldn't do it if he knew I was out with another man, so I thought of you."

"Sure, I don't have anything going on that night, but are you sure you want to have dinner with a man you hardly know? I mean he's a cop, right?"

"That's more of a reason to spend time with him. With Jim's deterioration and drinking, a cop would be a great protector."

"Protector? Clare! Do you even know anything about him?"

"He's kind, gives me compliments and he's so handsome. You should meet him." Clare took a bite of her baked chicken.

"I don't know if I want to meet him yet. Maybe if you have a good time on the date then I can check him out, but I'll wait and see how it goes."

"Okay, I'll fill you in after we have dinner on Friday. Do you want me to bring Kayla to your place or watch her here?"

"I'll watch her at your place just in case you get home late, then she can sleep in her own bed."

"That's fine with me. You are more than welcome to spend the night if you want."

"We'll see."

Clare explained about the house she went to clean and what she'd come across, including the detective and the picture, he'd shown her.

"Do you think this detective knows who's killing these women?"

"I shouldn't be telling you any of this. It is an ongoing case."

"I won't tell anyone, Clare. You know that."

283

"I know I can trust you, but here's a question for you. Why are you so interested in this case? Every time I tell you something new, you get, I don't know, nervous and defensive?"

"Nervous, how do you know if I'm nervous or not?"

"I can hear it in your voice, Brenda. You don't want me to get close to Detective Parks. It's as if you're hiding something from me." Silence filled the air between them. Clare didn't know if she said something wrong or if her suspicions were confirmed. "This murder thing is too much. I don't want it to come between us."

"You're right. It has nothing to do with us and our friendship, so let's just forget about it and move on with our lives. You have a wonderful dinner and I hope he is good to you. You deserve a loving relationship, Clare. And Kayla does too. If this guy makes you happy, then by all means I am happy for you."

"Thank you, Brenda. I want to be happy, but I'll never know if I don't get out there."

"You've got a point there, Clare. Well, I'd better sign off, need to get ready for work tonight. What time should I be there on Friday?"

"I'll have to get back to you on that." It was Wednesday and Detective Parks hadn't called her to confirm the time yet. She wondered if he'd changed his mind about going out with her.

"Okay, bye."

Clare hung up and finished her dinner before checking on Kayla who was sitting on the living room floor with her teddy bear in her arms watching TV; Clare smiled, then washed the dishes, and joined her daughter on the floor.

****

Hours later, Clare sat on the sofa after putting Kayla to bed and turned on the news to catch the weather—she didn't expect to see a picture of her friend staring back at her. She moved closer to the television as the news reporter stated that 'Dan McMinlow was killed in a bar fight.'

"He can't be dead!" Clare gasped. "Oh, Dan, what happened?" The reporter went on to say how he was murdered and that the men had stabbed him repeatedly. According to the witnesses at the bar, they said the victim was in the wrong place at the wrong time.

Tears rolled down her cheeks as she thought back over all the times they'd spent together. She couldn't take her eyes away from the screen, but Dan's picture faded as the reporter went on to other news.

She slid back against the sofa with her face in her hands; she couldn't stop crying.

All she could think about was how much she cared for Dan and he never knew it. She never had a chance to tell him. He didn't want a commitment and she didn't want to lose him as a friend.

"Now… now he's gone, and I'll never be able to see him." Her mind replayed every moment they spent together in slow motion; she closed her eyes and felt him beside her. She could hear his words as he told her, "Everything will be okay, Clare."

She opened a drawer in the nightstand next to her bed and pulled out the only picture she had of Dan. She held it to her chest and crawled into bed, crying herself to sleep.

Twenty-Nine

Clare

Waking the next morning, her eyes puffy, she padded into the kitchen for a cup of coffee. She couldn't stop thinking about the death of Dan. They just talked on the phone the other night and now she wouldn't be able to see him again. She fought back the tears while taking a sip of her coffee before getting dressed.

Later that day, Jim called her and asked to come over because he wanted to talk. She didn't want to see him, not after what he'd done to her at the store, but thought about Kayla and decided he could.

He didn't show up until 9:00 p.m. and Kayla was already fast asleep in her bed. *He would do that*, she thought. She was thankful she hadn't told Kayla he was coming over. She would have been heartbroken, again. She unlocked the door and opened it before he knocked a second time.

"Hey, Clare. How was your day?"

"Good, I guess," she replied, reaching for her neck.

"Why, what's wrong? Did I do something?"

Seriously, he's asking that? Does he not remember what he did to me yesterday? Does he not see the bruises on my neck? Clare couldn't believe it.

"Why are you looking at me like that, Clare?" he questioned as his eyes scoured the living room as if in search of something.

She followed him and took a seat on the overstuffed chair. "So, what did you want to talk about? I thought you would come over earlier so you could see Kayla, but I guess I was wrong."

"Oh, I'll spend some time with her this weekend, maybe take her on Friday and keep her for the weekend. If that's okay with you?" He sat on the arm of the chair and Clare felt herself recoil at his nearness.

"You want her for the weekend? That's not like you, but sure, I guess that's fine with me. What's the big occasion?" She scoped out the features of his face to search for a reaction.

"No occasion. Just want to spend some time with her."

Clare could sense he was hiding something; there was more to taking Kayla than he was letting on. *Could he be seeing someone and wants Kayla to meet her?* she thought, but instead of keeping her thoughts to herself, her mouth opened. "So, are you seeing someone? Is that why you want Kayla?"

"Where did that come from?"

"Are you?" She was curious why he would even lie to her. She didn't have a say on who he could date and she really didn't care, or did she? Is that why she was feeling this way — the final cut of the string and there'd be no more of them as a couple? No more family. After everything he'd said and done to her, she should be happy for him and glad he would leave her alone.

It's no wonder he always showed up after Kayla was in bed. He didn't want to see her: he wanted Clare. But why did he kiss her if he was seeing someone else? Didn't she want him to let go and move on with his life? She could try to deny she still had feelings for him, but they were feelings for the old Jim; not the one sitting beside her now. She knew she'd never have that Jim back again. She needed to snap out of this fantasy world she lived in. She didn't want or need his shit now. Not after last night: not after her friend being killed. She didn't even know if she should tell him that Dan had died. It was the end of Jim and Dan's friendship the last time they spoke, but only because Jim accused them of sleeping together — which of course didn't happen and now would never happen.

She decided not to say anything about Dan and to let Jim find out on his own. It's not like she had to tell him. Besides, if they were still friends, they'd have kept in contact with each other, but with everything that had happened she could understand why they didn't.

She couldn't help but feel angry with Jim for all the times he slept around and then turned on her. The sad part was, even though she had feelings for Dan, they never did anything about them, not like Jim and the women he'd been with.

Jim actually went as far as sleeping with them; drunk or not, he still did it. Shaking her head with disgust, she stood and headed out onto the porch. But before she could close the slider, Jim was right behind her. They sat outside with him smoking, but neither one spoke a word. The warm night air embraced Clare; she sat back wishing he'd just leave. Leave and never come back. For once, she wished he would be honest with her and not hide the fact that he was seeing someone. She needed to get him to talk and make him acknowledge that she didn't care, or at least make him think she didn't.

"Jim, you can tell me who she is. I'm not going to get irate and go to her house. We're friends now and Kayla's parents, that's all we are." Why was her heart breaking with the words she'd just said? She cared for this man sitting beside her: that's what it was. Why shouldn't she? She'd done everything for him, but he drank and slept around in return. He was the one who didn't care. He was the one who didn't respect the vows they had taken.

"Look, if it makes you feel better, I have a date on Friday. So, yes, you can have Kayla for the weekend."

"What do you mean, you have a date? Who is he? Do I know him?"

She was surprised how quick his attitude changed toward her.

"Like I said, I have a date on Friday. Is that okay with you?"

"No, it's not okay with me!" he shouted.

"Well, I'm sorry you feel that way, Jim. So, it's okay that you're seeing someone, but not me. I have the right to move on with my life too; besides, it's not like I planned it. It just happened and I said 'yes'." She almost didn't say yes to Detective Parks, but that was only because she didn't want to get hurt again. She wanted to hide in her shell forever, but what kind of life would that be for her daughter? She deserved to go out and have fun. What was she supposed to do, lock herself up, and not live her life? How would Kayla feel about not going out and meeting new people if Mommy sat at home because she didn't want to get hurt again? Sure, right now, she was too young to understand, but one day she will want to know why.

"I don't owe you any explanation, as much as you don't owe me one. You made your own choices, Jim, and I deserve to be happy too. What do you expect me to do? Be alone and not have a life?"

"Well, yes!"

Did he just say 'yes', that I'm not supposed to have a life, but he can? "Get out of my house, Jim! I don't want you here anymore, just leave." Clare opened the slider and pointed to the front door. "Just go, get out of here!"

Jim stood and stormed out towards the door. He reached to grab the knob and paused, then returned to the center of the room. "Do you think we can have one more night together, Clare? I promise, after tonight I won't ask you again." He began to move closer to her.

She tried to register the words he'd just spoken. *Did he just say what I think he said? He wants to jump into bed as if nothing has changed between us. Was he crazy?*

"You have the nerve to ask me for sex? Look, I just want you to leave; go and enjoy your life. Get out!" She stepped towards him, making him fumble backwards. Once he'd stepped beyond the door, she shut and locked it before he could react. Looking through the peephole, she could see him standing there.

"I'll be back, Clare. You have no right to a life. You have a daughter to raise and one day we'll be a family again. Just wait and see, I'll get you back." She hurried to her bedroom and peered through the window to watch him drive away. Sitting on the side of the bed she mumbled out loud, "He has the nerve to ask for sex?"

****

By the time Friday morning came, she thought only of Detective Parks. She tried to talk herself out of going a hundred times. *Am I even ready to date someone?* That, she wasn't sure of, but she knew she couldn't hide from herself or forget the ordeal Jim had put her through. She needed to find out if she was able to open up to another man. She'd made it through all those heartaches before and still loved again, so what would make this relationship any different? She knew who she had become when she was with Jim, but she couldn't go back and change that. She had given him her heart and she was angry and disgusted that he was unfaithful to her. The next guy wouldn't be that stupid to cheat on her and break her heart. At least she hoped not.

Thirty

Detective Parks

Detective Parks stretched his arms above his head and yawned. He couldn't shake the dream he'd just had. Pulling the blanket to his chest, he lay in bed thinking about Clare. It was a strange dream, he would have to admit that, but there was something about her that he couldn't define. In his dream, she was behind bars but not the bars you would see in a jail. These bars were different. It was like she was trying to get out and kept mouthing the words 'help me.' Like she was trapped. Thinking back to their conversation the other day, he remembered she had mentioned her husband and some of the things he'd done, but what did those things mean?

Ring. Ring.

Reaching over to the nightstand, he grabbed his cell phone and answered it.

"Hello."

"Hi, Detective Parks?"

"Yes. Who's calling?"

"It's Clare, Clare Culback."

He pushed down on the bed with his free hand and moved to a sitting position. "Well, hello, Clare. I was just thinking about you."

"You were?"

"Yeah, just going over what we talked about." He didn't want to tell her about the dream, at least not yet. "So, what's up?"

"I just thought I'd call and let you know that I found a sitter and we can go out tonight."

Smiling into the phone, he responded, "That's great, I'm looking forward to getting to know you a little better."

"Me too."

"Good, so what time do you want me to pick you up?"

"How about I meet you somewhere?"

"Are you sure? It's no problem if I pick you up, is it? But if you'd rather meet somewhere else? Or better yet, you could just drive over to my house and we can go together from here."

"That sounds good. I'll come to your place. I'll see you then. Oh, before I forget, what time do you want me to arrive?'

"Is 6:00 p.m. good?"

"How about closer to 7:00 p.m., I won't be off work until 5:00 p.m. and I have to pick up my daughter then take her to her dad's place."

"Sounds good, Clare. 7:00 p.m. it is."

He waited for her to hang up before setting the phone down on the table.

He spent the rest of the day working on his cases and making a run to the police station.

Last night he went back to both of the victims' homes and checked out the lighting in the parking lot. The witnesses were right about it being too dark to see the motorcycle.

After pulling into the station, he made his way to Detective Malarkey's office to see if the fingerprints had come back on the photos, but he wasn't in so he strolled down the hall to the lab. The prints belonged to Shannon and no other visible prints were found. There were no prints on the money that was left for Clare or on the SERVPRO cleaning product. He was actually surprised about the money not showing any prints, but the forensic analyst said it must have been washed before it was left there. He decided to run a trace on the SERVPRO to try and locate any buyers in the area who may have ordered some recently and then go from there.

Detective Malarkey poked his head into the lab. "Hey, Parks. I have those results back from the last victim. They're in my office."

"Okay, I'll be there in a sec. I just have a few things to look over." Minutes later he strolled down the hall, turning left at the third door. "Mind if I make some copies to take back to the house?" Detective Parks asked.

"No, go right ahead."

"So, let's see the results." Detective Parks reached across the desk.

"We got one hit on the prints, but the other tissue sample they took wasn't in CODIS, so it looks like we could have a possible suspect on our hands." As he browsed down the page, his eyes suddenly stopped.

"Shit."

"What's wrong? Did you find something? Parks, talk to me, man." Detective Malarkey leaned forward, staring at Parks.

"Just thinking how I'm going to handle this." He scanned over the results, hoping he'd read the report wrong.

"Handle what?"

"Never mind, I'll take care of it. Thanks for getting this to me." He stood up and moved to the door then waved goodbye.

Sitting in his car in the parking lot, he reread the results. "How am I going to handle this?" he said out loud, keeping in mind that there were two different results of the tissue found under the victims' nails: one he knew about, but the second wasn't in the system. Meaning, the other person hadn't committed any crimes to be put into the database yet. Parks had to do a little more research.

Back at the house, Detective Parks positioned himself in front of the computer. He wanted to find out everything about Clare's husband before their date tonight. He didn't want to ask her about him. Besides, she knew too much already and he didn't want her to get hurt.

He had hit a dead-end in the case, at least with Jim Culback; though that didn't mean anything, he could have still killed those women. Looking at Jim's record, Parks found he had one DUI and a driving under suspension. There were a couple of arrests that were made due to suicide attempts with a loaded gun. Jim was taken to Daniel Penning on Golden Gatte Road.

Making copies of the reports, Parks then decided to check out his record in Ohio and look for anything that may have happened up there. Reports showed that he was arrested five times for DUIs and multiple suicide attempts.

"Holy shit, this man is screwed up. How the hell does he even have a license? That's six DUIs since the age of thirty-one and not counting all the times he was put in a psycho ward. It's no wonder Clare is wary of me. After living with a man like that for years, who could blame her."

He went downstairs after printing the remaining documents and laid them out on the dining room table. He circled and highlighted everything that stood out about Jim. He even ran a DMV on him and highlighted all the vehicles he had owned at one time or the other. Opening the file from Ohio, he scanned through it to see if anything matched, but the only item he came across was a motorcycle Jim had owned in Ohio and the one down here in Florida. Without the model of the motorcycle, he couldn't pinpoint him as being there: not without sufficient evidence.

Hours later, a fax came in on the SERVPRO. There were two places in Naples that had purchased the product and they were both restaurants in the area. He did a route plan on the two, then grabbed his gun, holster, badge and wallet.

****

After pulling into the parking lot located near the rear of the building, he walked up the stairs. There was a small bar to the right of him with ten or more tables and chairs scattered on the patio. A sign was posted on the beam: *Outside patio. Open every evening after 6:00 p.m.*

To his left were two glass doors that led into the restaurant. As he opened the door smoke billowed out and the smell of fried fish and chicken enveloped him, causing him to gag. It wasn't just the smell of fried food that bothered him, but also the mixture of liquor in the air with cigarette smoke. The air was thick and even though he was a smoker himself, the smell in this place made him nauseous.

A waitress holding menus smiled at him and motioned for him to take a table, but he shook his head and asked to speak to the owner. Her smile fell flat. She turned on her heels and pushed into the swinging doors that led to the kitchen.

Moments later a short, plump man wearing a splattered apron, which could have been white at one time, swung the doors open and waddled towards Detective Parks.

"Can I help you with something?" the man asked.

"I hope you can. I'm Detective Parks and am investigating a homicide. I'll get to the point why I'm here. Have you or did you buy any cleaning products for your restaurant by the name of SERVPRO?" He knew the owner had bought the item, but he wanted to hear it from him.

"Sounds familiar, but I would have to get my order book and check."

"I'll wait here while you do that." He stared at the fat man, waiting for him to retrieve the book, but he just stood there eyeing Detective Parks up and down.

"Today would be nice," Detective Parks barked.

The man's face turned red as a cherry, he trotted off and returned minutes later with a book. Setting it on a table next to them, he flipped through the pages until he came across a list of cleaning products.

"The amount has been changed." The manager motioned for a woman behind the bar to join them. The obese man showed her the page and asked if she'd changed the amount ordered that day. She replied no and that she wouldn't change any orders he'd placed. "It seems that someone has changed the order, but I distinctly remember receiving the order and they only come in quantities of six."

"Do you mind looking for the box and seeing if there were six shipped in your order?" The wheezing man grabbed the book and waddled back into the kitchen. Detective Parks leaned against the wall waiting for him to return.

A couple of men sitting at the bar glanced over their shoulder, staring him down. "Is there a problem, gentlemen?" They both shook their heads and continued drinking their beers. One of the men stood up. He was thin and had short dark hair styled straight up at the front. Swaying, he made his way around the bar and followed the arrow to the restroom which pointed down the hallway.

"Hey, Jim, do you want me to order another beer for ya?" the man sitting at the bar asked.

"Sure, that would be great." The man, Jim, disappeared behind the corner, then returned moments later taking his seat at the counter again. He was startled when Detective Parks appeared next to him, making Jim spill his beer.

"Do you mind if I ask what your last name is?"

The man with dark hair and long eyebrows that connected on his forehead turned and looked him in the eye. "Why, what's it to you?" he said in his slurred, yet cocky voice.

"Just wanted to make sure you're not the man I'm looking for," Parks responded.

"Looking for? Why would you be looking for me?"

"You tell me, Jim."

"Look, I don't want any trouble. Can't you see I'm just sitting here having a few beers and relaxing? I wasn't bothering anyone."

"Then why won't you tell me your last name?"

"It's Culback. Jim Culback. Are you satisfied now, whoever you are?"

Detective Parks felt his stomach tighten as adrenaline raced through his veins. "Actually, I am. I've been looking for you. Do you have a few minutes to spare from your beer to go outside and talk?"

"What's this about?

"I'll tell you once we're outside." Detective Parks stood to the side and waited for Jim to exit his chair and stagger out of the front door.

"What's this all about? I haven't done anything wrong." Jim took a swig of his beer before taking a seat on the patio.

"I'm Detective Parks and I'm investigating the murder of two women you have been acquainted with recently." As he spoke, he watched Jim's body language to see how he reacted to the question.

"Look, I don't know what you've been told, but I didn't kill those women!"

He could tell Jim was hiding something. He watched perspiration roll down his face and onto his shirt.

"I don't know what you were told, but I'm innocent. I know I shouldn't have said what I did to Clare, but I'm telling you the truth. I didn't do it."

"Clare, what does this have to do with Clare? What did you say to her?"

"My question is, how do you know Clare and what did she say to you?"

"Listen, I ask the questions, not you!" Detective Parks snarled.

"I just want to know what information you have first before I say anything else," Jim answered back. "That's my right."

"We have evidence that you were with Shannon Crumb and Pam Grayer the night they were killed. I know that doesn't mean you killed them, but it doesn't look good from my point of view. If you don't want to talk, then I can arrest you and take you in for questioning. However, you want to handle this, is up to you."

"I think I need an attorney, but I can't afford one." Jim wiped the sweat on his forehead with a napkin from the counter.

The short, heavyset manager pushed open the glass door and confirmed that he did receive six bottles, but that two were missing and whoever took them had tried to cover it up by changing the order book. The man handed

Detective Parks a copy of the order sheet and turned to head back inside. Detective Parks dialed a number and a few minutes later a police cruiser showed up to take Jim into custody.

"I'll deal with you back at the station, Jim. I have some loose ends to tie up here first." Walking back inside, he talked to the short plump man about his employees and said that he wanted to question each one of them.

An hour passed and everyone that was working that day was interrogated. The other two women wouldn't be in until after 5:00 p.m. and the cleaning girl didn't come until 4:00 a.m. He told the manager that he'd be back later to speak to them. He also requested the cleaning girl's phone number. He then headed to the station to question Jim.

****

Watching Jim light a cigarette through the two-sided mirror and again wiping the sweat off his forehead, the detective noted Jim's leg was jittering like it was ready to race away from his body.

Opening the door to the interrogation room, Detective Parks walked in and took a seat in front of Jim. Laying the file down on the table, he studied Jim before opening it. He took some of the photos of Shannon and Pam out of the file and then fanned them out on the table.

He observed Jim as he looked at them and then saw him turn his head away in disgust. "What's wrong? Can't stand seeing what you did to them?"

"I didn't kill them, I told you that. There's nothing I can say that's going to change your mind." Jim puffed on his cigarette, stubbed it out and lit another one.

"Chain smoking? You must be hiding something. Talk to me, Jim, what happened on those nights when you went to their homes?"

Jim took in a deep breath. "What about an attorney? I thought I get one appointed to me if I can't afford one?" Detective Parks waved his hand at the mirror and seconds later a man carrying a briefcase entered the small room.

Reaching out his hand to Jim, he said, "Hi, I'm Attorney Gray and I will be representing you in this case." Jim shook his hand. Attorney Gray pulled out a chair and sat down next to Jim.

"Can you answer the question now, Jim? What happened on the night you went to Shannon's place?" Observing Jim's reaction, he jotted down Jim's answers on a yellow pad.

"I'm assuming you want the details of the last time I saw her?"

"If that's what you want to call it," Detective Parks returned.

"It was right after we moved to our new condo, just before Thanksgiving. She texted me, so I went to Shannon's place, then went home and we had dinner." Jim stubbed out his cigarette.

"Whose 'we'?"

"My wife Clare, me and our daughter."

"So, you're sleeping with someone behind your wife's back?" *What a scumbag. Now I know why Clare was pissed that day she found the photo*, Detective Parks thought.

"Yes, but I was ending it with Shannon. I didn't see her again after that night but I didn't kill her either. She was alive when I left." Jim tapped his index finger on the table.

"So, did you hear from her after that night? Did you tell her it was over?"

"No, actually she never did contact me after that night and yes, I told her I couldn't see her anymore," he answered, crossing his arms over his chest.

"And you didn't think anything of it?"

"No, I thought she took it well and respected my decision. It didn't even cross my mind, well, until I found out in May that her body was found on the beach."

"And how did you hear about it?"

"I was at an AA meeting with a group of others and they were talking about it. Before that I'd assumed she had accepted the breakup."

"Okay, so you say you ended it with her and got on with your life with Clare? What about Pam? When did she come into the picture?" Jim stared at the blinking red light on the camera sitting in the corner of the room.

"Pam, now, she was something special. I was going to leave Clare for her. It was the only way she'd be with me. Then Clare told me she was going to see a divorce attorney and, well, I changed my mind and broke it off with Pam."

"So, you wanted your cake and eat it too? Did you ever think how Clare would feel about you cheating on her?" Snapping his pencil in half, Detective Parks couldn't believe what an ass this Jim was; he felt sorry for Clare and what she'd had to endure.

"I love Clare and I was thinking that, well, I have no excuse for what I was doing, but I am sorry. And like I said, I didn't kill those women. Someone out there must be watching me and killing these women to frame me. I'm being set up."

"Set up. Like it's some kind of game? Is that what you're saying? Maybe you should just sit back, take a look at your life and stop betraying your wife and daughter. Think about them for a moment instead of yourself, but that's what you alcoholics do, right? Think of only yourselves." Feeling more irritated, Detective Parks again thought of Clare.

"Wait, how the hell do you know so much about me when this is the first time we've met? Who's telling you these things about me?"

"I ran a background check on you, Jim. I know everything about you. I know how many DUIs you have and the suicide attempts. I even know when you took your last shit. So, don't sit there all cozy and think I don't know jack shit about you! You can take that cocky attitude and stick it where the sun doesn't shine. I ask the questions, not you!"

Jim's face turned beet red as he stared into the detective's eyes. "Are we done here? Is there anything else you need to ask me? Because if not, I'm free to go," Jim huffed.

"No, there's nothing else, but don't think of leaving town. I might need to bring you in for further questioning." Detective Parks gathered his files and bolted from the room in disgust, leaving Jim with Attorney Grey.

Thirty-One

Jim

Minutes later, Jim pushed his chair back and left. Digging out his cell phone from his pants pocket, he went outside and texted Clare asking to meet her, but she didn't respond. Feeling more irritated, he remembered that his car was back at the bar and started to walk.

He couldn't believe the detective thought he was the one who had killed those women. "He knows I've slept with them, but he didn't believe what I had to say. I should just tell him what I know. I don't want to go back to jail. Fuck, what should I do?" he mumbled.

****

Forty-five minutes later, he stood by his car with a million thoughts racing through his head and the only way he could quiet them was to drown them out. He turned and sprinted up the stairs and into the bar.

Several hours later, he staggered to the restroom. After pissing for the third time, he wobbled back to his seat and dropped down. Thoughts of the interrogation came rushing back. He needed to see Clare and get things straight between them. Looking at his phone, he noticed that Clare had texted him. He texted her back, stating he needed to see her and where he was.

Thirty-Two

Clare

Clare couldn't believe he'd done it to her again. He was drinking instead of keeping his promise and taking Kayla for the weekend. How could she believe him and trust that he was different when he was still drinking?

It was almost 5:00 p.m., he was drunk and wanted her to come pick him up, once again. How many times had she stopped what she was doing and retrieved him from a bar because he was too drunk to drive? All the times when she had to carry Kayla, who was sleeping, out to the vehicle and go pick up his ass. When was it all going to end? He promised her that he'd take Kayla but it was just another broken promise.

After finishing the house she was cleaning, she drove to the restaurant/bar and called Brenda on the way but got her voicemail. She explained the situation and that she needed her to pick up Kayla from school. Then she called Detective Parks and left a message stating she had to cancel their date, explaining that the sitter she'd lined up had a change of plans so they'd have to reschedule for some other time.

Her heart raced. She gripped the steering wheel just to keep her hands from shaking. Pulling into the lot, she parked up. After taking several deep breaths, she opened the glass door and made her way inside. The air was filled with a fog of smoke and the smell of fried fish and liquor. Glancing around, she saw Jim sitting next to a woman in a red skin-tight dress with her boobs ready to pop out at any minute from the low-cut top. A hot rush passed through Clare as she stood staring at them. She walked over and tapped him on his shoulder. He turned to her.

"Hey, Clare. What are you doing here? Pull up a seat and have a drink with us?"

"What am I doing here!" she screamed. "You texted me to come get you, you asshole!" Smiling at the woman in the red dress, he winked and ordered another beer.

"Let's go, Jim! You've had enough to drink." Clare signaled to the bartender to ignore the beer he'd requested.

"Damn it, Clare! You always seem to ruin the party. Why can't you just loosen up and have some drinks with us." He pushed his stool back and stood up.

"I have a child to raise. She doesn't need two drunken parents! Or did you forget that you have a daughter?"

"Back off, Clare. You know I love her and that she means the world to me."

Clare laughed. "You have a funny way of showing her. I'm glad Kayla doesn't ask about you and wonder why her dad doesn't have time for her. It would break my heart to see her cry over you. Hell, I've done enough of that for the both of us!" She felt her eyes wanting to burn through his soul.

She turned and bolted through the two glass doors, leaving the fog of smoke inside. By the time she'd made it to her car, he'd grabbed her arm and spun her around.

"Leave me alone, Jim! You've done enough damage," she cried, twisting her arm from his grip. He punched her in the face, making her fall to the ground. Tears streamed down her cheeks as she touched the spot where he'd hit her. There was so much pain and she could feel her face swelling up around her eye.

She fumbled through her purse looking for whatever she could find to defend herself from him, then she heard a door slam a few cars down from them. The next thing she knew Jim was falling on her. That's when she saw her; her long blonde hair blowing in the evening wind.

"Angel, what are you doing here?" Angel pulled out the knife and stabbed him in the kidneys. She'd used the same knife on the other women she'd killed. She twisted the knife inside him, then pulled it out and repeatedly stabbed him until he was curled up on the ground.

"You will never hurt her again, Jim," Angel said, looking at Clare. "He's hurt you more than enough; he deserves to die, Clare."

Clare watched as blood poured from the wounds inflicted on him. Watching him take his last breath, she reached over and felt for a pulse.

There wasn't one.

Thirty-Three

Angel - Present time

"I wonder about Clare and how she is doing. I wonder what became of her since Jim's death. Is she happy? Did she and that detective ever get together? Does she know why I did what I did?

"Why did you kill those women and Jim?" the woman asked.

"There's a lot behind what I did for her. Being in here gives one time to think about life, but the truth is I'd do it again for her."

"But that doesn't explain why you killed those women. Why would you choose to live in here instead of out there, where you can make a difference?"

"Don't you get it? There isn't anything out there for me. She is my best friend and I would do anything for her. She deserves to have a life and be happy. He sure in hell wasn't going to let her be happy. She has a daughter that loves her and needs her! Men that lie and cheat don't deserve to live. Once a cheater, always a cheater—that's my philosophy. Men don't care who they hurt as long as they get what they want, when they want."

"Calm down, Angel. So, you killed those women and Jim because of what they did to your friend?"

"Yes. I've been in her situation before. People don't change. Men don't change. They say they will, but they all lie."

"Tell me what happened after you killed Jim?"

"As I watched him lying there in his own blood, I felt relieved for Clare. Now she can have a life and not worry about him hurting her or possibly killing her. The look on her face said it all. When she felt for his pulse and realized Jim was dead, I can honestly say she looked…relieved. That's when Detective Parks pulled in and saw us there. After taking me into custody, he took samples from me; all the evidence came together — the tissue sample matched and then I came here.

"Where does Brenda fit into all of this?"

"Yes, Brenda. I don't want to forget about her. One night I followed her to that bar, you know the one she cleaned every morning, and I made my way to the kitchen when she was busy working in the restrooms. I did what Detective Parks did: I searched and found where I could get my hands on some SERVPRO. If it weren't for that detective showing up when he did, I probably would have got away with it. I know Clare would have turned the other cheek."

"That doesn't explain how Brenda fits into all of this?"

"I needed to get into the building and how else but wait for her to arrive? She caught me stealing the SERVPRO. She knew who I was but knew to keep her mouth shut, or I would tell Clare everything.

"Tell her about what?"

"That Brenda was sleeping with Jim. That they were going to be together after the divorce was final, but…but that's one body they will never find."

"What happened to Brenda? What did you do with her?"

"Clare trusted her, but she betrayed Clare. She did the one thing she shouldn't have done: she slept with Jim. That night when he called her over, she actually did stay and watch a porno film with him. They continued to sneak around afterwards, even when Clare lived with her. It had to be done: she had to die."

"Well, Detective Parks said Jim freaked out when he saw the photos of Shannon and Pam. He looked surprised and disgusted by them."

"My plan was to make him crazy and maybe then he would take his own life. But he took too long, and I just couldn't wait. When I was out in the parking lot and saw him grab her, I had to stop him. I had to end his life."

"Well, I think that is all for today. I'll take you back to your room now." The woman waves her hand towards the mirror.

"There's one more thing I need you to do."

"What is it, Angel?"

"I have a letter for Clare. I would like you to give it to her. It will explain everything."

The woman nods.

A man comes into the small room and unlocks the braces that bind Angel's hands to the chair. They walk down the hall and he opens the door to the one place she will always call home.

Epilogue

Clare – Present time

I stare at the letter in my hand as tears fall down my face. I miss my friend Angel and wish she hadn't done what she did. The letter stated she was doing fine and that I should come and visit her soon. The words I read stung my heart and I couldn't believe that my entire relationship with Jim was a lie. Angel finished the letter by telling me about Brenda and Jim and what they were planning to do, but that I didn't have to worry about Brenda: she was gone too. She said she had killed all those women because she was tired of men cheating and abusing women. That she herself had been abused and would never be able to have a baby of her own. Her late husband had taken that away from her.

Angel had killed Jim because of that. She was taken to the station along with myself. I hadn't heard back from Brenda and called my friend Jillian to see if she could pick up Kayla from school.

After the funeral for Jim, I decided to seek therapy. I went twice a week for six months in Florida and then continued seeing a counselor when I moved to Chicago. I still continue to have nightmares about my life with Jim, but they are slowly dissipating. The demons I felt growing inside me when I was with Jim have now left.

Detective Parks and I spent time talking and getting to know each other. He flew down to see me for a week at a time every month, and then eventually Kayla and I moved up to Chicago to start a new life. I didn't think I could ever be happy again and to love someone with all my heart, but I was wrong. If anything, I love more now than I have ever loved before. To me, sometimes my life now feels like a dream and I don't want to wake up. I pinch myself on occasion just to double-check I'm really here.

Sometimes in life, you have to endure the hard times to arrive at the place you're meant to be. After all, of those times with Jim, I didn't think I'd ever be happy again. I thought what I had chosen was the way my life was going to be. But somehow, I found the strength to pull through and walk away to find happiness and love. I didn't have to worry about being afraid for Kayla or myself. We would be just fine and live a good life.

****

The bus arrives and tiny feet clatter towards me. Her two small arms wrap around my right leg, hugging me. I glance down and smile, Kayla is home from school.

"How was school today, sweetie?"

"Good, Mommy. I made a new friend today and she let me sit with her at lunch. My teacher is funny, she makes me laugh, and we played games in class today," Kayla replies.

"I told you that things would get better and you would make friends. There's nothing to be afraid of." I soothe my hand down her hair as we walk towards the house.

"Can I go play on the swing set now?"

"Sure you can, sweetie." She bolts into the backyard. I make my way inside and step out on the deck, watching her as she moves her legs up to the sky and then down. I couldn't help thinking back to the day when I taught her how to swing. I love listening to my daughter's laugh and seeing her happy: it's what matters most to me.

Still smiling, I fold the letter and stuff it in my back pocket. I would file it away somewhere safe.

My body shivers from the feel of a kiss on my neck. I turn and embrace him. "I love you, Mr. Parks."

"And I love you, Mrs. Parks."

Broken Promises

Sometimes when we least expect it, life does end in happy ever after.

About Broken Promises

This story was written about my life with an alcoholic. None of the murders occurred, but everything else was based on the life I once had with my ex-husband.

I moved up to Chicago five years ago with my daughter who was adopted by her stepdad in 2012. We live in a beautiful home filled with love and trust.

My life then was chaotic, and my mind was a jumbled mess. I have spent six years in counseling and have managed to stop thinking as a co-dependent does. For those of you who were or are now in a relationship with an alcoholic, there is a better life out there for you — if you are willing to leave and seek it out. You are not alone and don't have to stay with them. No one deserves to stay with someone who is abusive in any way; physical or verbal.

I was at a point in my life where decision making was extremely hard for me. I didn't know what I wanted and when I did, I wasn't sure how to get it, or if it was the right thing to do.

People like us feel that we have no right to be happy; that we don't deserve a love that is healthy and positive.

But that is what we are brainwashed to believe. Alcoholics are manipulative and only think of themselves and what they want, so we in turn are thinking negative things about ourselves.

Some people may take offense to this, but it's what I have learned when my mind finally became clear. The fog had been lifted after many sessions in therapy. My present husband is a wonderful man who loves me for me, allows me to be myself, and respects what I want out of life. He allows me to live my dreams and stands by me through the hard times and good.

My whole point is that everyone deserves to be happy because **no one**, and I mean **no one**, needs to stay in a relationship with any kind of abuse. Alcohol, drugs, physical or verbal. I had more verbal abuse with my ex than physical, and in turn, it screwed up my head. This is only what I believe, so don't be offended if your opinion is different. Verbal abuse can be much more damaging than physical. Bruises heal, but your mind may be damaged for life and it takes years, and I mean years, to start thinking differently again. To think like you should and not that you are worthless and incapable of doing things.

I have noticed that I have times when I become angry for no reason. It's like there's an evil side to myself. I have gotten better and I'm not as angry as I used to be. And it's usually something little that makes me upset and lash out. Afterwards, I would get done yelling and screaming and hide somewhere, then wonder what was wrong with me and why I'd get so defensive. It's because of what I went through and I want to protect my heart from getting hurt again. We co-dependents get defensive and bitter, and we know nothing else but to defend ourselves from harm; even if the other person isn't going to hurt us in the same way the abuser did.

There are many places that people like us can go to and get the help we need in order to make ourselves better. Counseling and therapy cost money, but there are places out there that don't ask for a lot. You can try going to Al-Anon where you can talk to people just like us and donate what you can afford. It is a non-profit organization for people living with or are involved in an abusive relationship.

My final thoughts to you are: Life is short and we have no idea when it will end. Everyone has a right to be happy and loved. If you can leave your abusive relationship, I wish you a better and happier life because it will be worth it in the end. Just be cautious on the choices you make in your life and don't choose the same kind of people again that you have tried hard to leave. But mostly, you are not alone. Find someone to talk to who will help you.

All my love and prayers go out to those that are or have been in my shoes. God Bless!

About the Author

Donna M. Zadunajsky has published seven children's books and this is her first debut novel.

She lives in Illinois but was born and raised in Bristolville, Ohio where her family stilt resides.

To find out more about the author and her books go to:
http://www.donnazadunajsky.com

www.ingramcontent.com/pod-product-compliance
Lightning Source LLC
Chambersburg PA
CBHW072343020726
47506CB00004B/985